> "Congress shall make no law ... abridging the freedom of speech, or of the press."

First Amendment to the US Constitution

The basic foundation of our democracy is the First Amendment guarantee of freedom of expression. The Opposing Viewpoints series is dedicated to the concept of this basic freedom and the idea that it is more important to practice it than to enshrine it.

OPPOSING VIEWPOINTS® SERIES

Labor Unions and Workers' Rights

Avery Elizabeth Hurt, Book Editor

GREENHAVEN
PUBLISHING

Published in 2020 by Greenhaven Publishing, LLC
353 3rd Avenue, Suite 255, New York, NY 10010

Articles in Greenhaven Publishing anthologies are often edited for length to meet page
requirements. In addition, original titles of these works are changed to clearly present
the main thesis and to explicitly indicate the author's opinion. Every effort is made to
ensure that Greenhaven Publishing accurately reflects the original intent of the authors.
Every effort has been made to trace the owners of the copyrighted material.

Cover image: a katz/Shutterstock.com

Library of Congress Cataloging-in-Publication Data

Names: Hurt, Avery Elizabeth, editor.
Title: Labor unions and workers' rights / Avery Elizabeth Hurt, book editor.
Description: First edition. | New York : Greenhaven Publishing, 2020. | Series: Opposing
viewpoints | Includes bibliographical references and index. | Audience: Grades 9–12.
Identifiers: LCCN 2019022812 | ISBN 9781534505957 (library
binding) | ISBN 9781534505940 (paperback)
Subjects: LCSH: Labor unions—United States—History—Juvenile
literature. | Labor—United States—History—Juvenile literature. | Industrial
relations—United States—History—Juvenile literature.
Classification: LCC HD6508 .L2353 2020 | DDC 331.880973—dc23
LC record available at https://lccn.loc.gov/2019022812

Manufactured in the United States of America

Website: http://greenhavenpublishing.com

Contents

Chapter 5: Should the Minimum Wage Be Increased?

The Importance of Opposing Viewpoints

Perhaps every generation experiences a period in time in which the populace seems especially polarized, starkly divided on the important issues of the day and gravitating toward the far ends of the political spectrum and away from a consensus-facilitating middle ground. The world that today's students are growing up in and that they will soon enter into as active and engaged citizens is deeply fragmented in just this way. Issues relating to terrorism, immigration, women's rights, minority rights, race relations, health care, taxation, wealth and poverty, the environment, policing, military intervention, the proper role of government—in some ways, perennial issues that are freshly and uniquely urgent and vital with each new generation—are currently roiling the world.

If we are to foster a knowledgeable, responsible, active, and engaged citizenry among today's youth, we must provide them with the intellectual, interpretive, and critical-thinking tools and experience necessary to make sense of the world around them and of the all-important debates and arguments that inform it. After all, the outcome of these debates will in large measure determine the future course, prospects, and outcomes of the world and its peoples, particularly its youth. If they are to become successful members of society and productive and informed citizens, students need to learn how to evaluate the strengths and weaknesses of someone else's arguments, how to sift fact from opinion and fallacy, and how to test the relative merits and validity of their own opinions against the known facts and the best possible available information. The landmark series Opposing Viewpoints has been providing students with just such critical-thinking skills and exposure to the debates surrounding society's most urgent contemporary issues for many years, and it continues to serve this essential role with undiminished commitment, care, and rigor.

The key to the series's success in achieving its goal of sharpening students' critical-thinking and analytic skills resides in its title—

Opposing Viewpoints. In every intriguing, compelling, and engaging volume of this series, readers are presented with the widest possible spectrum of distinct viewpoints, expert opinions, and informed argumentation and commentary, supplied by some of today's leading academics, thinkers, analysts, politicians, policy makers, economists, activists, change agents, and advocates. Every opinion and argument anthologized here is presented objectively and accorded respect. There is no editorializing in any introductory text or in the arrangement and order of the pieces. No piece is included as a "straw man," an easy ideological target for cheap point-scoring. As wide and inclusive a range of viewpoints as possible is offered, with no privileging of one particular political ideology or cultural perspective over another. It is left to each individual reader to evaluate the relative merits of each argument— as he or she sees it, and with the use of ever-growing critical-thinking skills—and grapple with his or her own assumptions, beliefs, and perspectives to determine how convincing or successful any given argument is and how the reader's own stance on the issue may be modified or altered in response to it.

This process is facilitated and supported by volume, chapter, and selection introductions that provide readers with the essential context they need to begin engaging with the spotlighted issues, with the debates surrounding them, and with their own perhaps shifting or nascent opinions on them. In addition, guided reading and discussion questions encourage readers to determine the authors' point of view and purpose, interrogate and analyze the various arguments and their rhetoric and structure, evaluate the arguments' strengths and weaknesses, test their claims against available facts and evidence, judge the validity of the reasoning, and bring into clearer, sharper focus the reader's own beliefs and conclusions and how they may differ from or align with those in the collection or those of their classmates.

Research has shown that reading comprehension skills improve dramatically when students are provided with compelling, intriguing, and relevant "discussable" texts. The subject matter of these collections could not be more compelling, intriguing, or urgently relevant to today's students and the world they are poised to inherit. The anthologized articles and the reading and discussion questions that are included with them also provide the basis for stimulating, lively, and passionate classroom debates. Students who are compelled to anticipate objections to their own argument and identify the flaws in those of an opponent read more carefully, think more critically, and steep themselves in relevant context, facts, and information more thoroughly. In short, using discussable text of the kind provided by every single volume in the Opposing Viewpoints series encourages close reading, facilitates reading comprehension, fosters research, strengthens critical thinking, and greatly enlivens and energizes classroom discussion and participation. The entire learning process is deepened, extended, and strengthened.

For all of these reasons, Opposing Viewpoints continues to be exactly the right resource at exactly the right time—when we most need to provide readers with the critical-thinking tools and skills that will not only serve them well in school but also in their careers and their daily lives as decision-making family members, community members, and citizens. This series encourages respectful engagement with and analysis of opposing viewpoints and fosters a resulting increase in the strength and rigor of one's own opinions and stances. As such, it helps make readers "future ready," and that readiness will pay rich dividends for the readers themselves, for the citizenry, for our society, and for the world at large.

Introduction

> "For a long time, the conventional wisdom was
> that wage growth had slowed because of rising
> competition from low-paid workers in foreign
> countries (globalization), as well as the replacement
> of workers with machinery, including robots
> (automation). But in recent years, economists have
> discovered another source: the growth of the labor
> market power of employers—namely, their power
> to dictate, and hence suppress, wages."
>
> —"More and More Companies Have
> Monopoly Power over Workers'
> Wages. That's Killing the Economy,"
> by Suresh Naidu, Eric Posner, and
> Glen Weyl, Vox, April 6, 2018

In an employer-employee relationship, the employer has a great deal of power. People must have jobs in order to feed their families. They need jobs that pay a living wage and offer benefits, such as health insurance and vacation time. They need jobs that provide safe working conditions. However, an individual worker has little bargaining power with a large employer. If an employee asks his employer to make changes to his workplace to make it safe, the employer has the power to fire that worker and hire another. Workers are especially at a disadvantage when unemployment is high, so employers can easily find replacement workers. Large, powerful employers also have a huge advantage over individual employees, in part because they can afford excellent legal counsel and long complex court battles should an employee sue them.

Unions are meant to address this imbalance of power. Unions are organizations of workers who join together to bargain collectively—rather than as individuals—for better wages, benefits, and working conditions.

The history of unions in the United States goes back almost to the founding of the nation. In 1791, Philadelphia carpenters organized a strike demanding a ten-hour workday. (Yes, the guarantee of having to work no more than ten hours a day was once a huge improvement.) However, it took a long time for unions to gain much power. In 1914, the Clayton Antitrust Act made it legal for employees to strike against their employers, giving unions power to back their demands.

Over the years, union membership and power has waxed and waned. Between the end of the Civil War and the 1920s, industry blossomed and so did unions. During the economic boom of the 1920s, unions lost a great deal of influence, as many people deemed them unnecessary in the strong economy. Then the Great Depression roared in. Jobs became scarce, so employers had far more power over workers than they'd had when workers had more jobs to choose from. They could offer unreasonably low wages and provide dangerous working conditions knowing that employees, desperate for jobs, had no choice but to accept their terms. In this environment, workers began returning to unions for protection and strength in numbers.

The New Deal—the package of legislation that addressed the Great Depression—included many protections for workers. In 1935, for example, the National Labor Relations Act (NLRA, also referred to as the Wagner Act) solidified some protections for unions by giving most workers (there were a few exceptions) the right to organize and join labor unions. This was a huge turning point for labor in the United States.

While many of the protections of the NLRA remain in force, the law was significantly weakened in 1947 by the Taft-Hartley Act, which made "closed shops" illegal. Closed shops are companies in which membership in a union is a condition of employment. Taft-Hartley also made it possible for states to enact controversial right-to-work laws, which make payment of union dues voluntary.

The perspectives in *Opposing Viewpoints: Labor Unions and Workers' Rights* prove that the conversation about unions and their role in American labor is as lively as it ever was. In chapter 1, "Are Unions Necessary?," you will read viewpoints that argue that unions are—once again—unnecessary, while others make the case for why unions are needed now more than ever. The viewpoints in chapter 2, "Are Labor Unions Good for the Economy and Workers?," take a close look at the question of whether organized labor helps or harms the economy. In chapter 3, "Do Unions Contribute to Political Corruption?," the viewpoints address the issue of corruption in labor unions—a criticism that has dogged unions for decades. Chapter 4, "Does Right-to-Work Protection Harm Workers?," takes on the debate, still raging today, over right-to-work legislation. And the final chapter, "Should the Minimum Wage Be Increased?," addresses not unions specifically but the debate over increasing the minimum wage.

As you will see, the debate over unions and other labor issues doesn't break down neatly across a left to right spectrum. The issues are complicated and often quite nuanced. Virtually all the authors represented here at least pay lip service to the value of unions in the past. After all, they point out, unions gave us weekends and over-time pay, and they ended child labor. The question the authors can't seem to agree on is whether organized labor—at least in its current form—is something the nation still needs. Are unions still making the world a better place? In this volume, you will find plenty of resources to jump start your thinking on this timely topic.

CHAPTER 1

Are Unions Necessary?

Chapter Preface

In one form or another, unions have played an important role in the United States for most of the nation's existence. Despite great resistance to the rise of unions in the 1920s and 1930s, most people today agree that unions are responsible for much of the nation's progress. Who can argue that the elimination of child labor and the establishment of a forty-hour work week were bad things? However, in recent times, support for unions has slipped and membership has dropped dramatically. The viewpoints in this chapter examine the reasons for this and the effects of the decline.

Some of the chapter's viewpoint authors see the decline in unions as beneficial. They argue that unions have become corrupt, that they hamper economic development, and that they depress wages and eliminate job opportunities for unskilled workers.

Other viewpoint authors see the loss of union power as a major setback for rights and hope for equality. They believe that unions created a strong middle class and provided a route to the middle class for African Americans. Thanks to the decline in unions, the current generation of African Americans and people of color, including many immigrants to the United States, no longer have this opportunity to get decent jobs that provide stability, decent wages, and benefits.

Are unions necessary? Are they still relevant? The viewpoints in the following chapter differ in their answers, but they all agree that, for better or worse, unions are in serious decline and that decline could have profound effects on the economy and society.

> "*Unions helped to counteract class-based inequality in political participation, ensuring that elected officials heard the policy desires of millions of non-elite Americans.*"

Unions Still Matter

Jake Rosenfeld

In the following viewpoint, Jake Rosenfeld discusses the history of the decline in labor unions before going on to analyze some of the achievements of organized labor over the years. These include increased wages, decreased racism and xenophobia among workers, and more civic participation by "non-elite" Americans. The author closes by discussing the challenges currently facing unions. Jake Rosenfeld is an associate professor of sociology at the University of Washington-St. Louis who specializes in the causes of inequality and determinants of wages and salaries.

"The Rise and Fall of US Labor Unions, and Why They Still Matter," by Jake Rosenfeld, The Conversation, March 27, 2015. https://theconversation.com/the-rise-and-fall-of-us -labor-unions-and-why-they-still-matter-38263. Licensed by CC BY-ND 4.0.

As you read, consider the following questions:

1. How does Rosenfeld say that unions also benefitted nonunion workers?
2. How, according to this viewpoint, do unions increase civic participation?
3. What are the challenges currently facing unions, according to Rosenfeld?

The US labor movement was once the core institution fighting for average workers. Over the last half century, its ranks have been decimated. The share of the private sector workforce that is organized has fallen from 35% to approximately 6.5% today.

An expanding body of research demonstrates just what this loss has meant: the growth of economic and political inequality, stalled progress on racial integration and the removal of an established pathway for immigrant populations to assimilate economically.

Yet despite their decline, unions in the US retain some power in certain pockets of the country. Recent successes by these organizations reveal the importance of a revitalized labor movement for the nation's economic and civic health.

What Went Wrong?

By the mid-1950s, unions in the US had successfully organized approximately one out of every three non-farm workers. This period represented the peak of labor's power, as the ranks of unionized workers shrank in subsequent decades.

The decline gained speed in the 1980s and 1990s, spurred by a combination of economic and political developments. The opening up of overseas markets increased competition in many highly organized industries. Outsourcing emerged as a popular practice among employers seeking to compete in a radically changed environment. The deregulation of industries not threatened by overseas competition, such as trucking, also placed organized labor at a disadvantage as new nonunion firms gained market edge through lower labor costs.

Simultaneously, US employers developed a set of legal, semi-legal and illegal practices that proved effective at ridding establishments of existing unions and preventing nonunion workers from organizing. Common practices included threatening union sympathizers with dismissal, holding mandatory meetings with workers warning of the dire consequences (real or imagined) of a unionization campaign and hiring permanent replacements for striking workers during labor disputes.

A sharp political turn against labor aided these employer efforts. President Reagan's public firing of striking air traffic controllers vividly demonstrated to a weakened labor movement that times had changed. Anti-union politicians repeatedly blocked all union-backed efforts to re-balance the playing field, most recently in 2008-2009, with the successful Senate filibuster of the Employee Free Choice Act. EFCA would have made private sector organization efforts somewhat easier. The last major piece of federal legislation aiding unions in their organization efforts passed in 1935.

Why Does It Matter?

At its peak, the US labor movement stood alongside powerful business leaders and policymakers as key institutions shaping the nation's economy and polity. Union workers enjoyed healthy union "wage premiums," or increases in pay resulting directly from working under a union-negotiated contract.

But nonunion workers also benefited from a strong labor presence.

In research by Harvard University's Bruce Western and myself, we compared nonunion workers in highly organized locales and industries to nonunion workers in segments of the labor market with little union presence. After adjusting for core determinants of wages, such as education levels, we found that nonunion workers in strongly unionized industries and areas enjoyed substantially higher pay. Thus the economic benefits of a powerful labor movement redounded to unorganized workers as well as union members.

Early 20th-century unions—especially craft unions—engaged in a range of sometimes violent discriminatory practices. As a result, in 1935, the year that President Franklin Roosevelt signed the Wagner Act, less than 1% of trade unionists were African American. While the Wagner Act extended basic organizing rights to private sector workers, millions of minorities remained unable to enjoy its protections by the actions of unions themselves. But throughout the second half of the 20th century, many unions shed these racist and xenophobic legacies.

In so doing, they opened up their organizations to African Americans eager to escape explicitly racist policies and practices common to many nonunion workplaces. African Americans soon had the highest organization rates of any racial or ethnic group, peaking at more than 40% for African American men and nearly 25% for African American women in the private sector.

These exceptional organization rates helped narrow racial pay disparities by raising African American wages. Had no union decline occurred from the early 1970s on, black-white wage gaps among women would be between 13% and 30% lower, and black males' weekly wages would be an estimated US$50 higher. Meanwhile, many immigrants and their children, echoing pathways taken by newcomers in generations past, such as the predominantly female, predominantly immigrant population of the International Ladies' Garment Workers' Union (ILGWU), used the labor movement as a springboard into the nation's middle class.

Unions' equalizing impact was not limited to the economic realm. A large body of research has found that union membership spurs civic participation among non-elite Americans. Voting, for example, is a practice strongly graded by income and education. More of either and Americans are much more likely to turn out to vote. Unions helped to counteract class-based inequality in political participation, ensuring that elected officials heard the policy desires of millions of non-elite Americans.

What Now for Labor?

The labor movement now finds itself in a peculiar period.

On the one hand, ongoing attacks by anti-union forces have crippled unions' organizational models in what were labor strongholds, including Wisconsin and Michigan. Many of these attacks have taken dead aim at what remains of labor's real strength: its public sector membership base.

Abetted by recent court decisions, efforts to defund and defang public sector unions are growing in size and sophistication by right wing policymakers and lobbying groups.

Curiously, despite serving as a primary source of votes and finances for the Democratic Party for much of the 20th century, labor finds itself with few political allies.

On the other hand, unions have enjoyed a series of recent successes at the state and local level. Movements to raise the minimum wage, offer paid sick leave to employees and pressure the largest private sector employer—Walmart—to raise its base compensation have all, of late, succeeded. These victories can be attributed, in part, to labor unions.

Unions provided much of the organizational and financial support that helped deliver these victories to millions of working Americans. Yet none of these wins translate directly into new dues-paying members.

Further successes on behalf of America's working- and middle-class appear limited unless unions discover a means to maintain its funding base. And without a revitalized labor movement, it is likely our inequality levels will remain at record highs.

> *"With these higher wages, unions bring less investment, fewer jobs, higher prices, and smaller 401(k) plans for everyone else."*

Unions Do More Harm Than Good

James Sherk

In the following viewpoint, James Sherk argues that unions are essentially cartels (an association of manufacturers designed to limit competition) that harm the economy, thus harming workers, both union and nonunion. He discusses both the economic and social consequences of unionization, concluding that, while unionizing does have the effect of raising wages—though perhaps minimally— these increases come at a steep cost, minimizing profits and returns on investments. James Sherk is a former Heritage Foundation fellow and, at the time of this writing, economic adviser to the Trump administration.

"What Unions Do: How Labor Unions Affect Jobs and the Economy," by James Sherk, the Heritage Foundation, May 21, 2009. Reprinted by permission.

As you read, consider the following questions:

1. In what ways do unions change the workplace, according to this viewpoint?
2. How, according to Sherk, have unions damaged the US auto industry?
3. Do you think the use of loaded terms such as "cartel" and comparisons with OPEC damage the author's argument?

What do unions do? The AFL-CIO argues that unions offer a pathway to higher wages and prosperity for the middle class. Critics point to the collapse of many highly unionized domestic industries and argue that unions harm the economy. To whom should policymakers listen? What unions do has been studied extensively by economists, and a broad survey of academic studies shows that while unions can sometimes achieve benefits for their members, they harm the overall economy.

Unions function as labor cartels. A labor cartel restricts the number of workers in a company or industry to drive up the remaining workers' wages, just as the Organization of Petroleum Exporting Countries (OPEC) attempts to cut the supply of oil to raise its price. Companies pass on those higher wages to consumers through higher prices, and often they also earn lower profits. Economic research finds that unions benefit their members but hurt consumers generally, and especially workers who are denied job opportunities.

The average union member earns more than the average non-union worker. However, that does not mean that expanding union membership will raise wages: Few workers who join a union today get a pay raise. What explains these apparently contradictory findings? The economy has become more competitive over the past generation. Companies have less power to pass price increases on to consumers without going out of business. Consequently, unions do not negotiate higher wages for many newly organized workers. These days, unions win higher wages for employees only at companies with competitive advantages that allow them to pay higher wages, such as successful research and development (R&D) projects or capital investments.

Unions effectively tax these investments by negotiating higher wages for their members, thus lowering profits. Unionized companies respond to this union tax by reducing investment. Less investment makes unionized companies less competitive.

This, along with the fact that unions function as labor cartels that seek to reduce job opportunities, causes unionized companies to lose jobs. Economists consistently find that unions decrease the number of jobs available in the economy. The vast majority of manufacturing jobs lost over the past three decades have been among union members—non-union manufacturing employment has risen. Research also shows that widespread unionization delays recovery from economic downturns.

Some unions win higher wages for their members, though many do not. But with these higher wages, unions bring less investment, fewer jobs, higher prices, and smaller 401(k) plans for everyone else. On balance, labor cartels harm the economy, and enacting policies designed to force workers into unions will only prolong the recession.

Push for EFCA

Organized labor's highest legislative priority is the misnamed Employee Free Choice Act (EFCA). This legislation replaces traditional secret-ballot organizing elections with publicly signed cards, allowing union organizers to pressure and harass workers into joining a union. EFCA would also allow the government to impose contracts on newly organized workers and their employers. Both of these changes are highly controversial.

Supporters defend EFCA by sidestepping concerns about taking away workers' right to vote. They argue that the bill will make it easier for unions to organize workers. They contend that unions are the path to the middle class and that expanding union membership will raise wages and help boost the economy out of the recession. The official case for EFCA rests on the argument that greater union membership benefits the economy.

Opponents of EFCA largely confine their critique to the legislation itself: its undemocratic nature and the problems with giving government bureaucrats the power to dictate work assignments, benefit plans, business operations, and promotion policies. They also argue, however, that increasing union membership will harm the economy.

Economists have exhaustively examined what unions do in the economy. When debating EFCA, Congress should look to the body of academic research to determine whether unions help or hurt the economy.

Unions in Theory

Unions argue that they can raise their members' wages, but few Americans understand the economic theory explaining how they do this. Unions are labor cartels. Cartels work by restricting the supply of what they produce so that consumers will have to pay higher prices for it. OPEC, the best-known cartel, attempts to raise the price of oil by cutting oil production. As labor cartels, unions attempt to monopolize the labor supplied to a company or an industry in order to force employers to pay higher wages. In this respect, they function like any other cartel and have the same effects on the economy. Cartels benefit their members in the short run and harm the overall economy.

Imagine that General Motors, Ford, and Chrysler jointly agreed to raise the price of the cars they sold by $2,000: Their profits would rise as every American who bought a car paid more. Some Americans would no longer be able to afford a car at the higher price, so the automakers would manufacture and sell fewer vehicles. Then they would need—and hire—fewer workers. The Detroit automakers' stock prices would rise, but the overall economy would suffer. That is why federal anti-trust laws prohibit cartels and the automakers cannot collude to raise prices.

Now consider how the United Auto Workers (UAW)—the union representing the autoworkers in Detroit—functions. Before the current downturn, the UAW routinely went on strike unless the Detroit automakers paid what they demanded—until recently, $70 an hour in wages and benefits. Gold-plated UAW health benefits for retirees and active workers added $1,200 to the cost of each vehicle that GM produced in 2007. Other benefits, such as full retirement after 30 years of employment and the recently eliminated JOBS bank (which paid workers for not working), added more.

Some of these costs come out of profits, and some get passed to consumers through higher prices. UAW members earn higher wages, but every American who buys a car pays more, stock owners' wealth falls, and some Americans can no longer afford to buy a new car. The automakers also hire fewer workers because they now make and sell fewer cars.

Unions raise the wages of their members both by forcing consumers to pay more for what they buy or do without and by costing some workers their jobs. They have the same harmful effect on the economy as other cartels, despite benefiting some workers instead of stock owners. That is why the federal anti-trust laws exempt labor unions; otherwise, anti-monopoly statutes would also prohibit union activity.

Unions' role as monopoly cartels explains their opposition to trade and competition. A cartel can charge higher prices only as long as it remains a monopoly. If consumers can buy elsewhere, a company must cut its prices or go out of business.

This has happened to the UAW. Non-union workers at Honda and Toyota plants now produce high-quality cars at lower prices than are possible in Detroit. As consumers have voted with their feet, the Detroit automakers have been brought to the brink of bankruptcy. The UAW has now agreed to significant concessions that will eliminate a sizeable portion of the gap between UAW and non-union wages. With competition, the union cartel breaks down, and unions cannot force consumers to pay higher prices or capture higher wages for their members.

Unions in Practice

Economic theory consequently suggests that unions raise the wages of their members at the cost of lower profits and fewer jobs, that lower profits cause businesses to invest less, and that unions have a smaller effect in competitive markets (where a union cannot obtain a monopoly). Dozens of economic studies have examined how unions affect the economy, and empirical research largely confirms the results of economic theory.

What follows is a summary of the state of economic research on labor unions.

Unions in the Workplace

Unionizing significantly changes the workplace in addition to its effects on wages or jobs. Employers are prohibited from negotiating directly with unionized employees. Certified unions become employees' exclusive collective bargaining representatives. All discussions about pay, performance, promotions, or any other working conditions must occur between the union and the employer. An employer may not change working conditions—including raising salaries—without negotiations.

Unionized employers must pay thousands of dollars in attorney's fees and spend months negotiating before making any changes in the workplace. Unionized companies often avoid making changes because the benefits are not worth the time and cost of negotiations. Both of these effects make unionized businesses less flexible and less competitive.

Final union contracts typically give workers group identities instead of treating them as individuals. Unions do not have the resources to monitor each worker's performance and tailor the contract accordingly. Even if they could, they would not want to do so. Unions want employees to view the union—not their individual achievements—as the source of their economic gains. As a result, union contracts typically base pay and promotions on seniority or detailed union job classifications. Unions rarely allow employers to base pay on individual performance or promote workers on the basis of individual ability.

Consequently, union contracts compress wages: They suppress the wages of more productive workers and raise the wages of the less competent. Unions redistribute wealth between workers. Everyone gets the same seniority-based raise regardless of how much or little he contributes, and this reduces wage inequality in unionized companies. But this increased equality comes at a cost to employers. Often, the best workers will not work under union contracts that put a cap on their wages, so union firms have difficulty attracting and retaining top employees.

Effect on Wages

Unions organize workers by promising higher wages for all workers. Economists have studied the effects of unions on wages exhaustively and have come to mixed conclusions.

Numerous economic studies compare the average earnings of union and non-union workers, holding other measurable factors—age, gender, education, and industry—constant. These studies typically find that the average union member earns roughly 15 percent more than comparable non-union workers. More recent research shows that errors in the data used to estimate wages caused these estimates to understate the true difference. Estimates that correct these errors show that the average union member earns between 20 percent and 25 percent more than similar non-union workers.

Correlation Is Not Causation

But these studies do not show that unionizing would give the typical worker 20 percent higher wages: Correlation does not imply causation. Controlling for factors like age and education, the average worker in Silicon Valley earns more than the average worker in Memphis, but moving every worker in Memphis to Silicon Valley would not raise his or her wages. Workers in Silicon Valley earn more than elsewhere because they have specialized skills and work for high-paying technology companies, not because they picked the right place to live.

Similarly, it is not necessarily unions that raise wages. They may simply organize workers who would naturally earn higher wages anyway. Unions do not organize random companies. They target large and profitable firms that tend to pay higher wages. Union contracts also make firing underperforming workers difficult, so unionized companies try to avoid hiring workers who might prove to be underperformers. High-earning workers do not want seniority schedules to hold them back and therefore avoid unionized companies.

Estimates from the Same Worker

Economists have attempted to correct this problem by examining how workers' wages change when they take or leave union jobs. This controls for unobservable worker qualities such as initiative or diligence that raise wages and may be correlated with union membership—the worker has the same skills whether he belongs to a union or not. These studies typically show that workers' wages rise roughly 10 percent when they take union jobs and fall by a similar amount when they leave those jobs.

Data errors become particularly problematic when following workers over time instead of comparing averages across groups. Some economists argue that these errors artificially diminish the union effect. More recent research explicitly correcting for measurement errors has found that taking union jobs causes workers' wages to rise between 8 percent and 12 percent. One Canadian study expressly examined how much of the difference between union and non-union wages was caused by unions and how much came from unmeasured individual skills. Over three-fifths of the higher wages earned by union members came from having more valuable skills, not from union membership itself. Just as the land surrounding Silicon Valley does not itself raise wages, most of the difference between union and non-union wages has little or nothing to do with unions themselves.

Wage Changes After Unionization

Studies tracking individual workers also do not prove that unionizing necessarily raises wages. Individual data do not account for firm-specific factors, such as large firms both paying higher wages and being targeted more commonly for organizing drives.

To discover the causal affect of organizing on wages, researchers compare wage changes at newly organized plants with wage changes at plants where organizing drives failed. Such studies look at the same workers and same plants over time, thereby controlling for many unmeasured effects. These studies come to the surprising conclusion that forming a union does not raise workers' wages. Wages do not rise in plants that unionize relative to plants that vote against unionizing.

Several of the authors of these studies have endorsed EFCA, but their research argues that expanding union membership will not raise wages. This should not come as a complete surprise. Unions in competitive markets have little power to raise wages because companies cannot raise prices without losing customers. Additionally, some unions—such as the Service Employees International Union—have expanded by striking deals promising not to seek wage increases for workers if the employer agrees not to campaign against the union.

Total Wage Effects

While economic research as a whole does not conclusively disprove that unions raise wages, some studies do come to this conclusion. It is difficult to reconcile these studies with the large body of other research showing that union members earn more than non-union members, or with the strong evidence that unions reduce profits.

A better summary of the economic research is that unions do not increase workers' wages by nearly as much as they claim and that, at a number of companies, they do not raise wages at all. Once researchers control for individual ability, unions raise wages between 0 percent and 10 percent, depending on the circumstances of the particular companies and workers.

Effect on Businesses

Union wage gains do not materialize out of thin air. They come out of business earnings. Other union policies, such as union work rules designed to increase the number of workers needed to do a job and stringent job classifications, also raise costs. Often, unionized companies must raise prices to cover these costs, losing customers in the process. Fewer customers and higher costs would be expected to cut businesses' earnings, and economists find that unions have exactly this effect. Unionized companies earn lower profits than are earned by non-union businesses.

Studies typically find that unionized companies earn profits between 10 percent and 15 percent lower than those of comparable non-union firms. Unlike the findings with respect to wage effects, the research shows unambiguously that unions directly cause lower profits. Profits drop at companies whose unions win certification elections but remain at normal levels for non-union firms. One recent study found that shareholder returns fall by 10 percent over two years at companies where unions win certification.

These studies do not create controversy, because both unions and businesses agree that unions cut profits. They merely disagree over whether this represents a feature or a problem. Unions argue that they get workers their "fair share," while employers complain that union contracts make them uncompetitive.

Which Profits Fall?

Unions do not have the same effect at all companies. In competitive markets, unions have very little power to raise wages and reduce profits. Companies cannot raise prices without losing business, but if union wage increases come out of normal operating profits, investors take their money elsewhere. However, not all markets are perfectly competitive. Unions can redistribute from profits to wages when firms have competitive advantages.

Economic research shows that union wage gains come from redistributing abnormal profits that firms earn from competitive advantages such as limited foreign competition or from growing demand for the company's products. Unions also redistribute the profits that stem from investments in successful R&D projects and long-lasting capital investments.

Consider a manufacturing company that invests in productivity-enhancing machines. Workers' output increases, and the company earns higher profits years after the initial investment. It has an advantage in the marketplace over companies that did not make that same investment. Unions redistribute the higher profits from this investment—not the normal return from operating a business—to their members.

Unions Reduce Investment

In essence, unions "tax" investments that corporations make, redistributing part of the return from these investments to their members. This makes undertaking a new investment less worthwhile. Companies respond to the union tax in the same way they respond to government taxes on investment—by investing less. By cutting profits, unions also reduce the money that firms have available for new investments, so they also indirectly reduce investment.

Consider General Motors, now on the verge of bankruptcy. The UAW agreed to concessions in the 2007 contracts and has made more concessions since then. If General Motors had invested successfully in producing an inexpensive electric car, and if sales of that new vehicle had made GM profitable, then the UAW would not have agreed to any concessions. The UAW would be demanding higher wages. After the union tax, R&D investments earn lower returns for GM than for its non-union competitors such as Toyota and Honda.

Economic research demonstrates overwhelmingly that unionized firms invest less in both physical capital and intangible R&D than non-union firms do. One study found that unions directly reduce capital investment by 6 percent and indirectly reduce capital investment through lower profits by another 7 percent. This same study also found that unions reduce R&D activity by 15 percent to 20 percent. Other studies find that unions reduce R&D spending by even larger amounts.

Research shows that unions directly cause firms to reduce their investments. In fact, investment drops sharply after unions organize a company. One study found that unionizing reduces capital investment by 30 percent—the same effect as a 33 percentage point increase in the corporate tax rate.

Unions Reduce Jobs

Lower investment obviously hinders the competitiveness of unionized firms. The Detroit automakers have done so poorly in the recent economic downturn in part because they invested far less than their non-union competitors in researching and developing fuel-efficient vehicles. When the price of gas jumped to $4 a gallon, consumers shifted away from SUVs to hybrids, leaving the Detroit carmakers unable to compete and costing many UAW members their jobs.

Economists would expect reduced investment, coupled with the intentional effort of the union cartel to reduce employment, to cause unions to reduce jobs in the companies they organize. Economic research shows exactly this: Over the long term, unionized jobs disappear.

Consider the manufacturing industry. Most Americans take it as fact that manufacturing jobs have decreased over the past 30 years. However, that is not fully accurate. Unionized manufacturing jobs fell by 75 percent between 1977 and 2008. Non-union manufacturing employment increased by 6 percent over that time. In the aggregate, only unionized manufacturing

Unions Price Low-Skill Workers Out of the Market

In 1948, the year I left home, the unemployment rate among black 16-year-olds and 17-year-olds was 9.4 percent, slightly lower than that for white kids the same ages, which was 10.2 percent.

Over the decades since then, we have gotten used to unemployment rates among black teenagers being over 30 percent, 40 percent or in some years even 50 percent. Such is the price of political "compassion."

Whatever the good intentions behind minimum wage laws, what matters are the actual consequences. Many people have ideological, financial or political incentives to obfuscate the consequences.

Labor unions are the biggest force behind attempts to raise the minimum wage, not only in the United States but in other countries around the world. That may seem strange, since most union members already earn more than the minimum wage. But the unions know what they are doing, even if too many gullible observers do not.

Low-skill workers with correspondingly low wages compete in the labor market with higher skilled union members with correspondingly higher wages. Many kinds of work can be done by various mixtures of low-skilled workers and high-skilled workers.

Minimum wage rates that are higher than what most low-skilled and inexperienced workers are worth simply price those workers out of the job markets, leaving more work for union members. All the unions have to do is camouflage what is happening by using rhetoric about "a living wage," or "social justice" or whatever else will impress the gullible.

Life was tough when all I could get were low-paying jobs. But it would have been a lot tougher if I couldn't get any job at all. And a tough life made me go get some skills and knowledge.

"Thomas Sowell on the Minimum/Living Wage and Why Labor Unions Support Raising Wages for Unskilled Workers," by Mark J. Perry, Pew Research Center, September 10, 2014.

jobs have disappeared from the economy. As a result, collective bargaining coverage fell from 38 percent of manufacturing workers to 12 percent over those years.

Manufacturing Employment: Union vs. Non-Union

Manufacturing jobs have fallen in both sectors since 2000, but non-union workers have fared much better: 38 percent of unionized manufacturing jobs have disappeared since 2000, compared to 18 percent of non-union jobs.

Other industries experienced similar shifts. Unlike the manufacturing sector, the construction industry has grown considerably since the late 1970s. However, in the aggregate, that growth has occurred exclusively in non-union jobs, expanding 159 percent since 1977. Unionized construction jobs fell by 17 percent. As a result, union coverage fell from 38 percent to 16 percent of all construction workers between 1977 and 2008.

Private Construction Employment:
Union vs. Non-Union

This pattern holds across many industries: Between new companies starting up and existing companies expanding, non-union jobs grow by roughly 3 percent each year, while 3 percent of union jobs disappear. In the long term, unionized jobs disappear and unions need to replenish their membership by organizing new firms. Union jobs have disappeared especially quickly in industries where unions win the highest relative wages. Widespread unionization reduces employment opportunities.

More Contractions but Not More Bankruptcies

Counterintuitively, research shows that unions do not make companies more likely to go bankrupt. Unionized firms do not go out of business at higher rates than non-union firms. Unionized firms do, however, shed jobs more frequently and expand less frequently than non-union firms. Most studies show that jobs contract or grow more slowly, by between 3 and

4 percentage points a year, in unionized businesses than they do in non-unionized businesses.

How can union firms both lose jobs at faster rates than non-union firms and have no greater likelihood of going out of business? Unions try not to ruin the companies they organize. They agree to concessions at distressed firms to keep them afloat. However, unions prefer layoffs over pay cuts when a firm does not face imminent liquidation. Layoffs at most union firms occur on the basis of seniority: Newer hires lose their jobs before workers with more tenure lose theirs. Senior members with the greatest influence in the union know that they will keep their jobs in the event of layoffs but that they will also suffer pay reductions. Consequently, unions negotiate contracts that allow firms to lay off newer hires and keep pay high for senior members instead of contracts that lower wages for all workers and preserve jobs.

Economists expect unions to behave like this. They are cartels that work by keeping employment down to raise wages for their members.

Consider General Motors. GM shed tens of thousands of jobs over the past decade, but the UAW steadfastly refused to any concessions that would have improved GM's competitive standing. Only in 2007—with the company on the brink of bankruptcy—did the UAW agree to lower wages, and then only for new hires. The UAW accepted steep job losses as the price of keeping wages high for senior members. If GM does file for bankruptcy, it will likely emerge as a smaller but more competitive firm. It will still exist and employ union members—but tens of thousands of UAW members have lost their jobs.

Unions Cause Job Losses

The balance of economic research shows that unions do not just happen to organize firms with more layoffs and less job growth: They cause job losses. Most studies find that jobs drop at newly organized companies, with employment falling between 5 percent and 10 percent.

One prominent study comparing workers who voted narrowly for unionizing with those who voted narrowly against unionizing came to the opposite conclusion, finding that newly organized companies were no more likely to shed jobs or go out of business. That study, however—prominently cited by labor advocates—essentially found that unions have no effect on the workplace. Jobs did not disappear, but wages did not rise either. Unless the labor movement wants to concede that unions do not raise wages, it cannot use this research to argue that unions do not cost jobs.

Slower Economic Recovery

Labor cartels attempt to reduce the number of jobs in an industry in order to raise the wages of their members. Unions cut into corporate profitability, also reducing business investment and employment over the long term.

These effects do not help the job market during normal economic circumstances, and they cause particular harm during recessions. Economists have found that unions delay economic recoveries. States with more union members took considerably longer than those with fewer union members to recover from the 1982 and 1991 recessions.

Policies designed to expand union membership whether workers want it or not—such as the misnamed Employee Free Choice Act—will delay the recovery. Economic research has demonstrated that policies adopted to encourage union membership in the 1930s deepened and prolonged the Great Depression. President Franklin Roosevelt signed the National Labor Relations Act. He also permitted industries to collude to reduce output and raise prices—but only if the companies in that industry unionized and paid above-market wages.

This policy of cartelizing both labor and businesses caused over half of the economic losses that occurred in the 1930s. Encouraging labor cartels will also lengthen the current recession.

Conclusion

Unions simply do not provide the economic benefits that their supporters claim they provide. They are labor cartels, intentionally reducing the number of jobs to drive up wages for their members.

In competitive markets, unions cannot cartelize labor and raise wages. Companies with higher labor costs go out of business. Consequently, unions do not raise wages in many newly organized companies. Unions can raise wages only at companies that have competitive advantages that permit them to pay higher wages, such as successful R&D projects or long-lasting capital investments.

On balance, unionizing raises wages between 0 percent and 10 percent, but these wage increases come at a steep economic cost. They cut into profits and reduce the returns on investments. Businesses respond predictably by investing significantly less in capital and R&D projects. Unions have the same effect on business investment as does a 33 percentage point corporate income tax increase.

Less investment makes unionized companies less competitive, and they gradually shrink. Combined with the intentional efforts of a labor cartel to restrict labor, unions cut jobs. Unionized firms are no more likely than non-union firms to go out of business—unions make concessions to avoid bankruptcy—but jobs grow at a 4 percent slower rate at unionized businesses than at other companies. Over time, unions destroy jobs in the companies they organize. In manufacturing, three-quarters of all union jobs have disappeared over the past three decades, while the number of non-union jobs has increased.

No economic theory posits that cartels improve economic efficiency. Nor has reality ever shown them to do so. Union cartels retard economic growth and delay recovery from recession. Congress should remember this when considering legislation, such as EFCA, that would abolish secret-ballot elections and force workers to join unions.

> "Unions and their benefits are
> especially important for communities
> of color, for whom unionization has
> long been a critical component of
> their economic mobility."

Unions Are Crucial If Workers of Color Are to Reach the Middle Class

Folayemi Agbede

In the following viewpoint, Folayemi Agbede explains how participation in unions was one of the ways African Americans gained access to the US middle class. These gains are not as available, says the author, for newer immigrants of color. Current efforts at union busting are driving people of color back down the wage scale, and keeping them in the middle class will require vigorous defense of unions. Folayemi Agbede is a strategist who served as special assistant for Progress 2050, a project of the Center for American Progress.

"The Importance of Unions for Workers of Color," by Folayemi Agbede, Center for American Progress, April 4, 2011. Reprinted by permission.

As you read, consider the following questions:

1. How are workers of color being shut out of jobs that pay decent incomes according to this viewpoint?
2. What benefits—in addition to pay—does the author say are more likely to be available to union workers than others?
3. What lessons can Latino immigrants learn from the African American experience with unions, according to the author?

Unions bolster opportunities for all workers in our country. They encourage political participation and offer access to the middle class, as a recent report from the Center for American Progress Action Fund explains. But unions and their benefits are especially important for communities of color, for whom unionization has long been a critical component of their economic mobility.

Workers who lack the collective leverage that unions provide are more distanced from the middle-class earnings and resources their unionized peers have, and this is particularly true for workers of color. Indeed, numbers show that most nonunion, nonwhite public-sector workers today fall farther below the median income of their white coworkers than they would with a union safety-net. And workers of color, including Native Americans, African Americans, Latinos, and Pacific Islanders, are often concentrated at the low-end of the wage spectrum—jobs which often benefit the most from the protection of unions.[1]

In lower-wage industries where union busting dramatically tempers access to competitive benefits, workers of color slide even farther down the wage scale. In the case of Wisconsin, and the impending attempts to decimate unions' collective bargaining power in Indiana and Ohio, people of color are increasingly being shut out of decent work and incomes because of weakened standards and lowered wage floors. These shutouts undermine the concentrated efforts that slowly inched workers of color toward closing the racial wealth gap that plagues low and middle-income people of color the most.

Although some wage gaps have been narrowed, it remains evident that the middle-class status-markers of competitive industry wages, comprehensive healthcare, and retirement benefits continually prove elusive for workers in lower-wage industries and public-sector work. Where workers of color are occupationally segregated—statistically crowded out of higher-wage, predominately white worker occupied jobs—available positions are decreasingly unionized (if at all) in addition to being low-income-earning positions with little to no benefits.[2] In this context, the success of unions in boosting socioeconomic mobility becomes inarguably apparent.

Without union leadership and protection, many people of color—with particular historical emphasis on African Americans—would not have accessed the middle class.[3] Black workers fought hotly contested, deadly fights for access to unions in order to secure basic protections and economic equity. The successful unionization of integrated workplaces over the last 140 years not only increased the wages of African Americans—who were otherwise making nickels to white workers dollars—but it also raised the overall floor for antidiscriminatory labor standards in hiring and benefit distribution. African-American workers collectively leveraged their arduous labor in exchange for safer conditions and better compensation by forming and joining unions— gaining standard protections historically denied to American workers descended of America's enslaved.

What gains African Americans have made through union protection and collective bargaining aren't as accessible for other groups because of diminishing unionization. On one hand, many Latinos, who have been in the United States for generations, have been able to leverage the same gains as their African-American counterparts by joining unionized workforces. On the other, as established and newer Latino communities continue to grow in the United States, many of the 23 million Latinos presently in the workforce stand a different, lower chance for middle-class means than they did in the past.

For new Americans, such as recent Latino immigrants and their first-generation American children, the concurrent decrease in unionization rates, the rise in Latino workforce growth, and Hispanic over-representation in low-wage work spells peril. The hard-fought access to unions that improved the economic standing for African-American workers could afford the same opportunities to immigrants and their children. In the absence of unions' protective force, however, transient workers searching for immediately available work signal to predatory employers that they are economically vulnerable and desperate.

In addition to having fewer economic levers, Latinos in the United States are less likely to have college degrees than white and African-American workers, and are crowded out of the increasingly college degree-based sector of good jobs. Where unions lower wage inequalities for workers without college degrees, the steady decline of unionization rates make Latino workers increasingly vulnerable in the quest for fair and beneficial employment.

Conclusively, without access to competitive pay in the public sector, collective bargaining and employer-provided benefits, the incomes of marginalized groups in the workforce would be even lower than their current amount. Workers of color's access to the middle class will be infinitely narrowed without unionization. This is why workers of color and their allies must defend unions in the face of a growing, state-by-state onslaught. Where unions are defended, they can be restored and improved by the fierce engagement of members of color. As unions reach a pivotal point in their American history, this is the time for workers who stand to lose so much to fight for them, win for them, and make them even better for the future.

Notes

1. Looking at the data, Asian workers tend to seem better off than white workers in wages because Asian communities are largely concentrated in states with high-costs of living. Therefore, the range of their median income is skewed by substantial population concentration in comparatively higher-wage states such as New York, California, and New Jersey. It remains true that public-sector workers are low- and middle-wage workers when compared to others in their areas.

2. There are gender and race differentials in wages within unions that are accounted for by a number of factors, including steering workers to lower paid nonmanagerial positions, discrimination in hiring, and promotional inequalities. All of this goes to say that unions are not infallible or immune to market discrimination, but they do keep historically marginalized workers from hitting economic floors.

3. "African American" also includes Caribbean and African persons who are not ethnically African American but also racially "black." These groups of immigrants and their American-born descendants have also benefitted directly from raised working standards although they still face much workplace exploitation in alternative economies.

> *"Why has the decline of American unions been so much more dramatic and precipitous than that of their European counterparts, given that both sets of countries have faced a similar set of economic challenges?"*

What Caused the Decline of Unions in America?

Dwyer Gunn

In the following viewpoint, Dwyer Gunn examines the causes for the decline in American unions during the second half of the twentieth century and analyzes why that decline was not nearly so steep in Europe. Many laws, beginning in the 1930s with the Taft-Hartley Act, have placed restrictions on American unions, Gunn explains, as has the lack of a consistently pro-labor political party in the United States. Dwyer Gunn is a journalist and former editor of Freakonomics.

"What Caused the Decline of Unions in America?" by Dwyer Gunn, the Social Justice Foundation, April 24, 2018. Reprinted by permission.

As you read, consider the following questions:

1. Why, according to this viewpoint, was the timing of Taft-Hartley particularly bad?
2. How did union foes use desegregation to increase opposition to unions in the Jim Crow South?
3. The author points out that in Europe most workers are covered by collective bargaining agreements, even when those workers are not in unions per se. How might this affect the strength of unions in those countries?

T he second half of the 20th century brought big, bold changes to the economic status quo in countries all over the world. Globalization and the invention of new technologies meant that companies in developed nations could produce goods for much less money in far-away factories or at home with the help of sophisticated machinery.

These forces undoubtedly explain part of the decline in union density and influence in the United States; fewer workers employed in the union-dominated manufacturing sector meant fewer union workers. But this decline has not been replicated to the same extent in many European countries. In Iceland, for example, 92 percent of workers are still members of a union, according to the most recent edition of the Organisation for Economic Co-operation and Development's *Economic Outlook*, an annual publication reviewing economic conditions and trends in developed countries. In the Scandinavian countries—Sweden, Denmark, and Finland—union density hovers around 65 percent.

Even in those European countries where union membership is lower, a much higher percentage of workers are covered by collective bargaining agreements. While union membership is only around 10 percent in France (much lower than the OECD average), almost 100 percent of workers are covered by collective bargaining agreements. In most of Europe, collective bargaining agreements are sector or industry-wide, covering vast groups of workers who aren't union members.

The diverging experiences of European and American unions raises a puzzling question: Why has the decline of American unions been so much more dramatic and precipitous than that of their European counterparts, given that both sets of countries have faced a similar set of economic challenges?

Often, when academics discuss the decline of unions in America, they point to the 1970s, a decade of sharp declines in union density, as the turning point.

Joseph McCartin, the executive director of the Kalmanovitz Initiative for Labor and the Working Poor at Georgetown University, has spent much of his career studying the history of organized labor in the US. McCartin believes that, to truly understand the roots of the decline of unions in America, you have to go back farther, to the post-World War II years.

That era brought two notable failures for unions: the passage of the Taft-Hartley Act and the failure of a coordinated campaign to unionize the South.

The passage of the Taft-Hartley Act in 1947 placed significant restrictions on unions, most of which still exist. It prohibited secondary boycotts and "sympathy" boycotts and opened the door to the right-to-work laws—which prohibit employers from hiring only union employees—that now exist in 27 states around the country. The legislation also required that union leaders sign affidavits swearing they weren't Communist sympathizers; refusal to sign meant they would lose many of the protections guaranteed by the Wagner Act, the landmark 1935 labor law that established the National Labor Relations Board and guaranteed workers the right to organize.

The Taft-Hartley Act came at a particularly inopportune time. Labor unions were in the middle of "Operation Dixie," a campaign to organize the non-unionized textile industry in the South. Anti-union business leaders in the region used the accusation that the leadership of some of the industrial unions were Communists, or Communist-leaning, to whip up opposition to Operation Dixie. Union foes also relied on another particularly powerful bogeyman—desegregation—to increase opposition to the industrial unions among white workers in the Jim Crow South. In one publication, typical of the time, distributed by the Southern States Industrial Council, one article asked "Shall We Be Ruled by Whites or Blacks?" and others alluded to the creeping threat of communism to traditional values.

In the face of this opposition, Operation Dixie ultimately failed—the Southern textile industry remained un-unionized.

"If there's any one moment that set the stage for later developments, I think it was that failure in the post-war years to continue the union growth that happened in the '30s and during the war," McCartin says. "Once there became a region of the country that wasn't unionized, it became a lot harder. When you compare us to France or Germany, there wasn't really a region of one of those countries where unions were just totally frozen out. The union movement was geographically hemmed in in this country—that turned out to be really, really costly."

Against this backdrop of vulnerability, the larger economic forces of the 1970s and '80s were devastating. The high inflation of the 1970s prompted Chairman of the Federal Reserve Paul Volcker to pursue a course of aggressive interest rate increases that increased the value of the dollar and decreased US exports, decimating the manufacturing sector. Unemployment skyrocketed, reaching 10.8 percent in 1982. Layoffs were common—21.2 percent of blue-collar workers experienced an involuntary job loss between 1981 and 1983.

In the face of such instability, companies found that workers in the manufacturing sector were both more willing to accept lower wages than they might have previously been, and more receptive to warnings that unionization campaigns could jeopardize their job security.

Meanwhile, popular sentiment in the country around economic policy was shifting. In the face of wage stagnation, Americans started to demand lower taxes, and resentment for public-sector workers grew. Politicians of both parties threw their support behind deregulation and free market reforms, arguing that only the forces of the free market could end stagflation and unleash the kind of innovation needed to improve living standards for all.

There have, over the years, been legislative efforts to restore unions to a measure of their former glory.

In 1965, labor groups mounted an effort to repeal the section of the Taft-Hartley Act that allowed state-level right-to-work laws, with the support of President Lyndon B. Johnson. It was successfully filibustered in the Senate. In 1978, another effort to reform labor law and institutions was also successfully filibustered. Likewise, a 1994 effort to pass legislation blocking employers from hiring permanent replacements for striking workers also died in the Senate. In an article in the *American Prospect* published in 2010, Harold Myerson argued that even President Barack Obama (widely viewed as the most labor-friendly president in years) abandoned the labor movement by not fighting hard enough for the Employee Free Choice Act in 2009, which would have made it easier for workers to form unions and increased fines on employers who violate labor law.

These failures highlight another difference between European and American unions. In many of the Western European countries where unions have maintained their strength, the relationship between organized labor and political parties takes two forms: unions either enjoy broad-based support from politicians across the political spectrum, or they have an extremely close relationship with one political party that consistently advances their priorities.

Consider, for example, the experience of Germany as compared to that of the US, where Republicans have been fiercely opposed to unions since the '70s.

"In Germany, the [German Trade Union Confederation, a trade union, also known as] DGB is non-partisan, their leaders talk with [Chancellor Angela] Merkel, they are not seen as a political enemy of the conservative party," says Richard Freeman, an economics professor at Harvard University who has studied unions for decades. "At one point, Republicans were not anti-union, but now the Republican Party sees unions as political enemies. And that means that whenever the Republicans get in power, they do everything possible to weaken the unions."

Nor does organized labor in the US have the type of tight relationship with the Democratic Party that labor unions in other countries (e.g. Sweden) enjoy with certain political parties. Democrats have, after all, proven themselves to be unreliable allies. In the 1970s, Democratic mayors won praise for various "strike-breaking" initiatives with respect to municipal initiatives, and the party has also supported the deregulation or privatization of previously heavily unionized industries like the sanitation, print, and telecommunications industries.

"In the US, there was never a durable labor party, and it does matter," McCartin says. "The Democratic Party became labor's more congenial ally, but it was never really all in. When priorities had to be set, the Democratic Party's willingness to prioritize labor was never quite there. Historically, that happened repeatedly. That made it hard for unions to advance a public policy agenda."

But as much as all of these factors explain some of the precipitous decline of unions in this country, many of the experts I interviewed for this article also pointed to something bone-deep in the American psyche, dating all the way back to the country's founding, that has simply made the country less fertile ground for labor unions.

Even simple geography played a role in shaping a different kind of corporate culture in America. America is simply much bigger than many European countries, which employers worried made it harder to construct the kind of stable, mutually beneficial relationships between labor and capital that are common elsewhere. "The market was big, and the competitive forces were stronger here than anywhere else—that shaped business culture," McCartin says.

Against this backdrop of a vast country filled with "Wild West" markets untethered from a national bureaucracy, business in

America also evolved in an environment in which the government was never seen as a partner, as it is in many European countries. Janice Fine, a professor at Rutgers who studies unions and alternative labor organizations, points out that, in Europe, the government played a valuable role in the early development of some industries and infrastructure, a history that lessened corporate hostility to regulation, such as those protecting workers' rights.

"In a lot of those countries, there isn't the same hostility to regulation because there's the sense that the state is a partner," Fine says. "But here, for a long time, business just was kind of free to do its own thing, and so it views regulation, when it does come, as holding it back."

"Ironically, it is partially the unions' role in helping to pass these federal laws that has led to their decline; workers began to find unions less important after many of their basic rights began to be protected under federal laws."

Unions Made Themselves Unnecessary

Katey Troutman

In the following viewpoint, Katey Troutman argues that unions are no longer doing the good that they did in the past. Troutman's reasons, however, are somewhat different from those of previous viewpoint authors. She argues that unions have accomplished so much in terms of legislative protections for workers' rights that much of the public believes unions are no longer necessary. This lack of public support has made it difficult for unions to continue to fight for progress for American workers. Troutman makes the case that stronger unions could play a role in ending income inequality. Katey Troutman is a journalist who writes for the Cheat Sheet.

"Top 4 Reasons Why People Say Today's Unions Are a Joke," by Katey Troutman, the Cheat Sheet, May 4, 2015. Reprinted by permission.

As you read, consider the following questions:

1. What achievements does the author mention as part of unions' legacy?
2. How, according to this viewpoint, are unions caught in a "vicious cycle"?
3. What are some things listed here that unions are no longer doing? How important are these?

Last year, the percentage of working Americans who were unionized reached a ninety-seven-year low, and public opinion of labor unions has been in the gutter throughout much of the past decade. Yet, labor unions have played an important role in US history, and some experts have suggested that the time is nigh for unions to make a comeback.

Public opinion of unions has declined in recent decades, particularly throughout the recession, but the most recent data shows the that trend might be changing, albeit slowly. A poll conducted late last month at Gallup concluded that most Americans (53%) now approve of labor unions. The 1950s saw unions' highest rate of approval, at 75%.

The labor movement has existed in one form or another in the United States since very early on in the nation's history. Indeed, unions have even played a number of crucial roles in the country's development. And while Americans' public opinion of labor unions has waxed and waned throughout the years, more recently the thinking seems to be that unions simply aren't relevant anymore.

Yet, despite the unions struggle to win over public opinion, they do boast an important legacy. For instance, the National Labor Union, which was created in 1866, played a critical role in convincing Congress to limit the work day. Labor unions are also responsible for federal laws such as the establishment of child labor laws, such as the Fair Labor Standards Act. Labor unions were also critical in the amendment of that law, the Equal Pay Act of 1963.

Ironically, it is partially the unions' role in helping to pass these federal laws that has led to their decline; workers began to find unions less important after many of their basic rights began to be protected under federal laws. *TIME* magazine notes that the low-levels of union membership in the United States today are also due to a kind of "vicious cycle" which has been turning for decades. "As unions decline, fewer people see their fates bound with unions, which just accelerates the decline."

But regardless of public opinion, there are some good reasons why Americans don't seem to think that unions are as crucial to their well-being as they once did. Simply put, unions need to do more for Americans. At the same time, Americans need to embrace a new, re-imagined version of the labor movement if it is to succeed.

The *Harvard Business Review* recently noted that there are a number of things unions used to do for Americans that they simply don't do anymore. Here are some of the biggest issues affecting American unions.

1. Unions No Longer Equalize Incomes

The *Harvard Business Review* notes that while it's true that income inequality remains much lower among unionized workers than it does among non-unionized workers, todays unions simply don't encompass enough Americans to make much of an impact.

Unionized workers still enjoy higher wages. In 2012, for instance, the median weekly income for union workers was $943, compared with just $742 for nonunion workers. But when unions are strong, they have a much wider sphere of impact. *TIME* magazine notes that, "when unions are stronger the economy as a whole does better. Unions restore demand to an economy by raising wages for their members and putting more purchasing power to work, enabling more hiring."

Right now, though, just 11% of Americans are unionized, so even if the unionized workers are making more, the unions are still not helping the majority of Americans. The *Harvard Business*

Review notes that the rise of income inequality since the 1970s is, at least in part, due to the steady decline of labor unions.

2. Unions No Longer Counteract Racial Inequality

Throughout much of their history, the *Harvard Business Review* notes, unions were very much racist institutions: For instance, most unions refused membership to African American workers, and some even worked to keep employers from hiring non-white workers.

Eventually though, labor unions in the US began to change, and by the 1970s, a profound shift had occurred and there were more unionized African American workers than there were unionized white workers. Labor unions are largely credited with helping to shepherd a new wave of African Americans into the middle class during this time, as well as helping to shrink the income gap between white and black Americans at the time.

Nowadays, income inequality between black and white Americans has widened again, particularly among women. Black women currently make about 64 cents to the white man's dollar, whereas white woman make 77 cents to that same dollar. Latina women have it even worse: They make just 56 cents to the white man's dollar.

3. Unions No Longer Play a Big Role in Assimilating Immigrants

While unions historically haven't been great to immigrants either, the labor movement has really dropped the ball with more recent waves of Spanish-speaking immigrants, save for a few smaller unionization campaigns throughout the Southwest.

Overall, the *Harvard Business Review* notes, Hispanic workers are much less likely to be unionized than non-Hispanics, despite the fact that the wage gap is often felt most acutely among Hispanic populations.

The *Review* does note that there have been a few notable exceptions in the form of unionization campaigns among immigrants, such as the United Farm Workers in California and the Service Employees International Union.

4. Unions No Longer Give Lower-Income Americans a Political Voice

In the past, unions were probably the most important organized interest group for working class Americans in Washington. But today, unionized workers are more affluent than they were in decades past, while the groups most in need of representation remain largely non-unionized. Pair that with the steady decline of unions overall and you're left with a sad political fact: Not only do unions not have much clout in Washington anymore, but they also don't necessarily represent the lower classes anymore.

The argument against a strong labor movement in the US in the past few decades has generally been based upon a pretty black and white idea that strong unions naturally result in less competitiveness. But in his article, Justin Fox notes that some of the most heavily unionized countries in the world, "Denmark, Finland, and Sweden, where more than 65% of the population belongs to unions … also perennially score high on global competitiveness ratings."

Stronger unions, it seems, could be one key to ending the income inequality that has received so much press over the past few months, and maybe, just maybe, Americans should re-think their ideas about labor.

> *"If there was no union apparatus to prop up wages, working people would find themselves more or less in free-fall, eventually dropping all the way down to the federal minimum wage."*

Working People Need Unions to Represent Their Interests

David Macaray

In the following viewpoint, David Macaray imagines what the United States would look like without labor unions. The author argues that without labor unions, workers would have no leverage to ensure they made a fair wage and labored under acceptable conditions. He makes the case that nearly every industry has trade organizations or professional advocates to represent and protect their interests, but most employees do not. Unions, he says, serve that purpose. David Macaray was a union rep and is now a playwright and author.

As you read, consider the following questions:

1. How does the author respond to the criticism that unions exploit workers by living off membership dues?
2. How does the author compare unions to lobbyists?
3. What does the author mean by "reverse gravity"?

"What Would a Country Without Labor Unions Look Like?" by David Macaray, CounterPunch, December 21, 2012. Reprinted by permission.

What would a country without unions look like? Before answering, we should clarify labor's role, both historically and presently. The purpose of a labor union is and always has been to raise the standard of living for working people. Simple as that. And by "standard of living" we mean wages, benefits, and working conditions, all of which are acknowledged by federal labor law to be legitimate topics for discussion in collective bargaining.

Of course, anti-labor propagandists like to pretend that unions are cesspools of greed, corruption and ineptitude, and that the only things they care about are consolidating power and living high on the hog off the membership's monthly dues. That's the rancid and misleading version of unions they try to peddle. Unfortunately, misleading version or not, many people believe it.

Take my case, for example. I was president of a local union for nine one-year terms, representing 700 employees at a Fortune 500 manufacturing plant. Although we were hard-working, dedicated employees, we were also a fairly militant union who wasn't averse to going on strike when the company got stingy. Hard-working employees and frisky union members … a perfect combination.

Monthly dues were roughly $30, and my salary during my first term was $100 per month. By the end of my ninth and final term, it had risen to $150. Admittedly, compared to the salaries of local presidents across the country, mine was probably on the low side. The average was closer to $200. Still, even at $200, no local president was living large.

If there were no unions, working people would have no means of resistance. Obviously, having no means of resistance is tantamount to having no leverage, and without leverage—without some form of bargaining power—we become sheep. If there were no unions, the arrangement would devolve into your classic "buyers' market," with management in the driver's seat, and working men and women along for the ride.

Historically, market forces tend to push wages downward. If there was no union apparatus to prop up wages, working people would find themselves more or less in free-fall, eventually dropping all the way down to the federal minimum wage of $7.25 per hour (which, if you worked 8 hours a day, 40 hours a week, 52 weeks a year, and never missed a day, pencils out to $15,080 per year).

As for the minimum wage, a significant portion of the Republican Party, along with the US Chamber of Commerce, would like to repeal it, believing the minimum wage to be an "artificial constraint," and the people who rely on it to be more or less "takers," too afraid or too lazy to take their chances in a free and open market.

Virtually every industry in the country—from bottle cap manufacturers, to cauliflower growers, to guided missile makers—has lobbyists or trade organizations representing their interests. What do working men and women have in the way of lobbyists? Other than unions, nothing. Other than unions, nothing and no one.

Indeed, even with unions, they usually find themselves out-manned, out-spent, and out-gunned, which is why the accusations of unions being "too powerful" are so ludicrous. People have actually said to me with a straight face, "Unions were necessary back in the old days, but now they've gotten too powerful."

Really? Too powerful? Here's a stunning fact: Only about 7-percent of all private sector jobs are unionized. Consider that figure. Seven-percent!! That means that 93-percent of all private sector jobs in the United States are non-union. Yet anti-union propagandists continue to portray organized labor has this gigantic, rampaging monolith.

It's no wonder that statistics show the American middle-class continuing to disintegrate at an alarming rate, and the top 2-percent continuing to get richer every year. The fact that the rich are getting richer makes eminent sense when you consider that, without any resistance, everything is going to be funneled upwards. Why wouldn't it? Think of the phenomenon as "reverse gravity."

Moreover, if there were suddenly no unions, even those well-paying non-union jobs out there would soon decline in quality as well. Why? Because with America's businesses no longer having to compete with union wages, benefits, and working conditions, they would be free to jettison whatever the hell they wanted, and the whole enterprise would quickly become a race to the bottom.

Again, this is all about leverage. It's all about resistance and maintaining a healthy standard of living, and it's all about our once vaunted middle-class being systematically assaulted and bled-out, and the country being transformed into one vast gladiatorial arena where everyone is treated as either a winner or loser.

In the 1950s, the US was prosperous, optimistic, and buoyant with confidence. During that period union membership was a staggering 34-percent. Today, we're struggling, polarized, and pessimistic. And union membership barely moves the needle.

Yet you still hear people—not just conservative pundits and free market fundamentalists, but regular working folks—blame the unions for our problems. It's true. Regular, good-hearted working folks are now hostile to the only institution capable of representing their interests. How bizarre is that?

Periodical and Internet Sources Bibliography

The following articles have been selected to supplement the diverse views presented in this chapter.

Angela Allan, "40 Years Ago, *Norma Rae* Understood How Corporations Weaponized Race," *Atlantic,* March 2, 2019. https://www.theatlantic.com/entertainment/archive/2019/03/norma-rae-40th-anniversary-racial-solidarity-unions-labor-movement/583924.

Laurent Belsie, "Labor-Union Militancy Revives, from Hotels to Schools and Steel Mills," *Christian Science Monitor*, October 25, 2018. https://www.csmonitor.com/Business/2018/1015/Labor-union-militancy-revives-from-hotels-to-schools-and-steel-mills.

Laura C. Bucci, "The Public Does Not Hate Labor," Jacobin, March 14, 2019. https://jacobinmag.com/2019/03/labor-union-support-state-level-opinions.

Oren Cass, "American Workers Need a New Kind of Labor Union," *Wall Street Journal*, August 31, 2017. https://www.wsj.com/articles/american-workers-need-a-new-kind-of-labor-union-1504220896.

Kavi Guppta, "Will Labor Unions Survive in the Era of Automation?" *Forbes*, October 12, 2016. https://www.forbes.com/sites/kaviguppta/2016/10/12/will-labor-unions-survive-in-the-era-of-automation/#2f7d24243b22.

Raymond Hoggler, "What's Behind the Decline of American Unions?" *New Republic*, November 30, 2016. https://newrepublic.com/article/139078/whats-behind-decline-american-unions.

Thomas Kochan, "Time to Reinvent Labor Unions for the Twenty-First Century: We Don't Need the Unions of Yesterday," Salon, September 3, 2016. https://www.salon.com/2016/09/03/it-is-time-we-reinvente_partner.

Dan Kopf, "Union Membership in the US Keeps on Falling, Like Almost Everywhere Else," Quartz, February 5, 2019. https://qz.com/1542019/union-membership-in-the-us-keeps-on-falling-like-almost-everywhere-else.

Alessandra Molito, "This Is How Much the Decline in Labor Unions Has Cut the Pay for All Workers." MarketWatch, August 23, 2018. https://www.marketwatch.com/story/this-is-how-much-the-decline-in-labor-unions-has-cut-the-pay-for-all-workers-2018-08-23.

Rick Moran, "Are Labor Unions Still Necessary?" *American Thinker*, September 4, 2017. https://www.americanthinker.com/blog/2017/09/are_labor_unions_still_necessary.html.

CHAPTER 2

Are Labor Unions Good for the Economy and Workers?

Chapter Preface

Many of the viewpoints in this chapter are deeply informed by the Great Recession, the devasting financial crisis that began in 2008 and from which the economy took nearly a decade to recover. Once the economy was booming again, commentators and experts found themselves confronting a strong economy that nevertheless seemed to have left American workers behind. Corporate profits boomed as wages and salaries stagnated. The gap between the rich and everyone else in the United States continues to grow. The middle class struggles to hang on. Even more than a decade after the crisis, the economy seems to be in a precarious state.

Workers responded to the post-recession situation by turning back toward unions. Though union membership didn't increase dramatically, union activity did. In 2018, according to the US Bureau of Labor and Statistics, there were 20 major work stoppages involving 485,000 workers. This was the largest number of workers involved in work stoppages since 1986. Corporations responded by using their considerable financial resources and political clout to make it difficult for workers to form unions and easier for corporations to get away with resisting them.

No one is seriously debating the fact that US workers are in trouble and that the economy, though apparently in good shape, is resting on shaky ground. However, there is a great deal of debate over whether unions could help solve these problems or make them worse. From the perspective of the top, the economy is doing just fine even in a time of weakened unions. From below, times of economic hardship are not good times to challenge powerful employers.

The viewpoints in this chapter take a variety of perspectives on these issues, from arguing that unions are the solution to virtually all the nation's economic woes to proclaiming that unions have become obsolete, if not dangerous to both the economy and to the workers who form and join them.

> *"Throughout the middle part of the 20th century—a period when unions were stronger—American workers generated economic growth by increasing their productivity, and they were rewarded with higher wages. But this link between greater productivity and higher wages has broken down."*

Unions Are Good for the Economy

David Madland and Karla Walter

When the following viewpoint was written, the United States was reeling from the financial crisis of 2008 and was at the beginning of the worst economic decline since the Great Depression. Authors David Madland and Karla Walter explore how falling wages can exacerbate recessions. They argue that by ensuring better wages for the middle class, unions can help create a strong and sustainable economy. David Madland is a scholar specializing in economics and the author of Hollowed Out: Why the Economy Doesn't Work Without a Strong Middle Class. *Karla Walter is a research analyst and director of the American Worker Project at the Center for American Progress.*

"Unions Are Good for the American Economy," by David Madland and Karla Walter, Center for American Progress, February 18, 2009. Reprinted by permission.

As you read, consider the following questions:

1. What, according to Madland and Walter, is the essence of what labor unions do?
2. What is the connection between wages, purchasing power, and the economy?
3. How, according to this viewpoint, does unionization reward workers for increased productivity?

The essence of what labor unions do—give workers a stronger voice so that they can get a fair share of the economic growth they help create—is and has always been important to making the economy work for all Americans. And unions only become more important as the economy worsens.

One of the primary reasons why our current recession endures is that workers do not have the purchasing power they need to drive our economy. Even when times were relatively good, workers were getting squeezed. Income for the median working age household fell by about $2,000 between 2000 and 2007, and it could fall even further as the economy continues to decline. Consumer activity accounts for roughly 70 percent of our nation's economy, and for a while workers were able to use debt to sustain their consumption. Yet debt-driven consumption is not sustainable, as we are plainly seeing.

What is sustainable is an economy where workers are adequately rewarded and have the income they need to purchase goods. This is where unions come in.

Unions paved the way to the middle class for millions of American workers and pioneered benefits such as paid health care and pensions along the way. Even today, union workers earn significantly more on average than their non-union counterparts, and union employers are more likely to provide benefits. And non-union workers—particularly in highly unionized industries— receive financial benefits from employers who increase wages to match what unions would win in order to avoid unionization.

Unfortunately, declining unionization rates mean that workers are less likely to receive good wages and be rewarded for their increases in productivity. The Employee Free Choice Act, which is likely to be one of the most important issues debated by the 111th Congress, holds the promise of boosting unionization rates and improving millions of Americans' economic standing and workplace conditions.

Unions Help Workers Achieve Higher Wages

Union members in the United States earn significantly more than non-union workers. Over the four-year period between 2004 and 2007, unionized workers' wages were on average 11.3 percent higher than non-union workers with similar characteristics. That means that, all else equal, American workers that join a union will earn 11.3 percent more—or $2.26 more per hour in 2008 dollars—than their otherwise identical non-union counterparts.

Yet union coverage rates have been declining for several decades. In 1983, 23.3 percent of American workers were either members of a union or represented by a union at their workplace. By 2008, that portion declined to 13.7 percent.

American Workers' Wage Growth
Lags as Productivity Increases

Workers helped the economy grow during this time period by becoming ever more productive, but they received only a small share of the new wealth they helped create. Throughout the middle part of the 20th century—a period when unions were stronger— American workers generated economic growth by increasing their productivity, and they were rewarded with higher wages. But this link between greater productivity and higher wages has broken down.

Prior to the 1980s, productivity gains and workers' wages moved in tandem: as workers produced more per hour, they saw a commensurate increase in their earnings. Yet wages and productivity growth have decoupled since the late 1970s. Looking from 1980 to 2008, nationwide worker productivity grew by 75.0 percent, while workers' inflation-adjusted average wages increased by only 22.6 percent, which means that workers were compensated for only 30.2 percent of their productivity gains.

The cost of benefits—especially health insurance—has increased over time and now accounts for a greater share of total compensation than in the past, but this increase is nowhere near enough to account for the discrepancy between wage and productivity growth. For example, according to analysis by the Center for Economic and Policy Research, between 1973 and 2006 the share of labor compensation in the form of benefits rose from 12.6 percent to 19.5 percent.

If American workers were rewarded for 100 percent of their increases in labor productivity between 1980 and 2008—as they were during the middle part of the 20th century—average wages would be $28.53 per hour—42.7 percent higher than the average real wage in 2008.

Unionization Rewards Workers for Productivity Growth

Slow wage growth has squeezed the middle class and contributed to rising inequality. But increasing union coverage rates could likely reverse these trends as more Americans would benefit from the union wage premium and receive higher wages. If unionization rates were the same now as they were in 1983 and the current union wage premium remained constant, new union workers would earn an estimated $49.0 billion more in wages and salaries per year. If union coverage rates increased by just 5 percentage points over current levels, newly unionized workers would earn an estimated $25.5 billion more in wages and salaries per year. Non-union workers would also benefit as employers would likely raise wages to match what unions would win in order to avoid unionization.

Increased Unionization Would Boost Americans' Annual Wages

Union employers are also significantly more likely to provide benefits to their employees. Union workers nationwide are 28.2 percent more likely to be covered by employer-provided health insurance and 53.9 percent more likely to have employer-provided pensions compared to workers with similar characteristics who were not in unions.

Conclusion

Nearly three out of five survey respondents from a Peter Hart Research Associates poll report that they would join a union if they could, but workers attempting to unionize currently face a hostile legal environment and are commonly intimidated by aggressive antiunion employers. The Employee Free Choice Act would help workers who want to join a union do so by ensuring fairness in the union selection process with three main provisions: workers would have a fair and direct path to join unions through a simple majority sign-up; employers who break the rules governing the unionization process would face stiffer penalties; and a first contract mediation and arbitration process would be introduced to thwart bad-faith bargaining.

Passing the Employee Free Choice Act and making it harder for management to threaten workers seeking to unionize would be good for American workers. It would help boost workers' wages and benefits. And putting more money in workers' pockets would provide a needed boost for the US economy. Increasing unionization is a good way to get out of our current economic troubles.

> "*Labor's decline squeezes the middle class, raises inequality, and undermines democratic values.*"

Unions Strengthen Both the Economy and Democracy

Harley Shaiken and David Madland

In the following viewpoint, Harley Shaiken and David Madland argue that unions are good for the economy and go one step further to make the case that they are also good for democracy. This viewpoint was written in 2008, when the Employee Free Choice Act was being considered in the US Congress. This was the name of several pieces of legislation over the years that would make it easier for employees to form unions and more difficult for employers to suppress unionization activity. As of this writing, the legislation has not passed. David Madland is a senior fellow and the senior adviser to the American Worker Project at American Progress. Harley Shaiken is a labor economist and specialist on issues of work, technology, and global production.

"Issue Brief: Unions Are Good for the Economy and Democracy," by Harley Shaiken and David Madland, Center for American Progress, December 9, 2008. Reprinted by permission.

As you read, consider the following questions:

1. How do the authors argue that unions create more motivated workers?
2. The authors explain that Henry Ford was able to cut the price of the Model T by paying workers more. How was this possible?
3. What was the Wagner Act, and how did it affect labor?

I t is good for the economy and good for American democracy when workers join together in unions, despite the claims of some conservatives who are waging a campaign to block important legislation that would make it easier to join a union.

Only 12 percent of American workers are currently represented by unions, and those who attempt to unionize face an uphill battle. The Employee Free Choice Act, which is likely to be one of the most important issues debated when the 111th Congress starts in January, holds the promise of restoring workplace democracy for workers attempting to organize, boosting unionization rates, and improving the economic standing and workplace conditions for millions of American workers.

The bill has previously passed the House and received majority support in the Senate, though the opposition of a few conservatives in the Senate has prevented the bill's final passage. Yet next year the bill has a very strong chance of becoming law due to the election of several progressive senators in November and President-elect Barack Obama's promises of support.

Consider these facts:

Unions Are Good for All Workers

They improve wages, benefits, and working conditions, and helped create the middle class.

Unions Raise Wages for All Workers

Unions paved the way to the middle class for millions of workers and pioneered benefits along the way, including paid health care and pensions. Even today, union workers earn significantly more on average than non-union counterparts and union employers are more likely to provide benefits. Workers in low-wage industries, women, African-American, and Latino workers have higher wages in unionized workplaces. Even non-union workers—particularly in highly unionized industries—receive financial benefits from employers who increase wages to match what unions would win in order to avoid unionization.

Without Unions, Fewer Workers Get Ahead

Shrinking union membership hurts all Americans. Corporations rather than workers are increasingly rewarded for growth in the economy. Long before the current financial crisis began, working families were struggling to make ends meet. American productivity has expanded by nearly 16 percent since 2001, but most of that economic boom bypassed workers, and real wages have remained flat. Corporate profits have meanwhile doubled since 2001, according to Moody economist Mark Zandi. Not since the 1920s has the link between economic growth and the well-being of the middle class been so tenuous. Labor's decline squeezes the middle class, raises inequality, and undermines democratic values.

Unions Are Good for the Economy

They can help foster a competitive high-wage, high-productivity economic strategy.

Higher Wages Are Competitive

Critics argue that union wages are too high and make it hard for American employers to compete globally. Yet competitiveness is also linked to productivity, quality, and innovation—all of which can be enhanced with higher wages. Henry Ford found in 1914 that paying employees $5 per day—double the auto industry's prevailing wage—reduced turnover, allowing him to cut the price of the

Nobody Likes Strikes, but All of Us Need Them

Nobody likes strikes; least of all unions. I'm an organiser, as was my dad and his dad before him. Organised workers do not actually gather in smoke-filled rooms, cackling over the prospect of crippling the economy and blowing up inflation like a beach ball. Workers want to keep earning, they want to keep working, but when you've exhausted asking, pleading, cajoling, negotiating and demanding in order to get a fairer shake for what your labour is worth, you're not left with a lot of other options but to strike. Essentially, it's management that causes strikes to happen, as has been the case throughout history.

The long, long list of things we enjoy today—minimum wage, weekends, overtime pay, sick leave, an end to child labour, and so much more—would not have been possible had it not been for workers who went on strike. You don't think bosses just altruistically and heroically let rain down their generosity over the toiling masses out of the goodness of their hearts, do you? No, working people had to strike, fight, sometimes even die for all the awesome stuff we take for granted today.

"Strikes Are Good for Us All," by Paul Fontaine, Fröken Ltd, May 13, 2015.

Model T and increase profits significantly. Ford commented that the $5 day was one of the finest cost-cutting moves we ever made.

Unionization and High Worker Productivity Often Go Hand-in-Hand

Fairness on the job and wages that reflect marketplace success contribute to more motivated workers. Given the pressures of globalization and competitiveness today, unions have been responsive to increasing productivity and embracing new innovations. In the retail world, labor costs in 2005 for partially unionized retailer Costco were 40 percent higher than Sam's Club, but Costco produced almost double the operating profit per hourly employee in the United States—$21,805 per employee versus $11,615 per employee.

Unions Are Good for Democracy

They give workers a voice on the job and in politics, and have been essential to the passage of some of the most important legislation of the past 100 years.

Unions Improve Communication
Between Workers and Managers

Unions give workers a voice on the job and improve communication between workers and management. Without unions, day-to-day competitive pressures leave quitting as the only option for workers to address serious problems—an expensive solution for all concerned.

Unions Have Helped Pass Important
Legislation That Helps All Americans

In the political arena, unions have pressed for improved minimum wages, health care coverage, retirement plan protections, overtime pay, and social security. When workers are able to join together in a democracy, the voice of workers can help balance out the power of business interests.

Unions Foster Political Participation

Unions are democratic membership organizations and foster the political participation of their members. They educate their members about the political process and train them how to work together for a common goal.

The Employee Free Choice Act Is Needed

Under current law, workers are often denied workplace freedoms and face a Herculean task joining a union.

Workers Attempting to Unionize Are Often Intimidated

Workers attempting to unionize face a hostile legal environment and aggressive antiunion employers. Expensive antiunion campaigns often seek to influence workers' votes by using threats—sometimes that the wrong vote could cost workers their jobs—one-on-one pressure, and mandatory meetings. One out of five union organizers or activists is likely to be fired during union election campaigns.

The Current Law Is a Failure

Labor law contains few penalties for employers who routinely harass, intimidate, and even fire people who try to join a union. Even after a vote in favor of unionization, employers often exercise their available rights of appeal and engage in bad-faith bargaining as a delay tactic that can go on for years.

Workers Want to Join Unions

Only 12 percent of American workers today are members of unions—but that's not because they don't want to be. A December 2006 Peter Hart Research Associates Poll reports that 58 percent of non-managerial American workers would join a union if they could.

The Employee Free Choice Act Would Restore Workers' Voices

The bill would make joining a union and getting a first contract fairer and easier.

The Employee Free Choice Act Promotes Workers' Rights

The bill would reform the labor-relations system to restore workers' basic democratic right to make a free choice to join a union.

The Employee Free Choice Act Is Fair

It would ensure fairness in the union selection process through three main provisions: workers would have a fair and direct path to join unions through simple majority sign-up, employers who break the rules governing the unionization process would face stiffer penalties, and a first contract mediation and arbitration process would be introduced to thwart bad-faith bargaining.

The Employee Free Choice Act Is Democratic and Restores Previously Won Rights

The bill would allow workers to join a union through simple majority sign-up or an election—as previous labor law allowed.

The Employee Free Choice Act Allows Majority Sign Up for an Election

The bill would allow an employee to choose to join a union through simple majority sign-up—a system that works well at the small number of workplaces that choose to permit it. The act does not deny workers their right to vote in a union election, as some conservatives maintain, but rather allows workers to choose between signing a membership card and having an election.

Workers Won Rights in 1935

Workers won important collective bargaining protections over 70 years ago with the passage of the Wagner Act. The Wagner Act placed the federal government squarely on the side of collective bargaining and the right to organize. An employer's duty was to remain completely neutral in a representation election, in recognition that economic dependence defines the relationship between employers and workers. Employer persuasion could not be separated from employer coercion.

The Wagner Act Promoted Majority Sign Up

Elections were just one way for workers to unionize during the 1930s. The National Labor Relations Board only required an election when genuine questions arose around a majority sign-up process. Almost a third of all union certifications between 1938 and 1939 occurred without an election according to labor historian Dr. David Brody, and under these legal rules millions of workers exercised their basic democratic rights, pouring into unions. Unfortunately, important safeguards requiring employer neutrality during union selection processes began to be dismantled starting in the 1940s. The Taft Hartley Act took away the NLRB's right to certify unions with simple majority sign up in 1947—employers from that point on could recognize their workers' petition, or request an additional election—where rules favor the employer.

The Employee Free Choice Act is necessary to restore workers' rights, boost the wages and benefits of Americans, and strengthen our economy. Passing the bill would help restore workplace democracy for workers attempting to organize, boost unionization rates, and improve the economic standing and workplace conditions for millions of American workers.

> "*Labor unions and the general public almost totally ignore the essential role played by falling prices in achieving rising real wages. They see only the rise in money wages as worthy of consideration.*"

Labor Unions Stifle Workers' Wages

George Reisman

In the following viewpoint, George Reisman argues that contrary to popular belief, labor unions effectively hinder economic opportunity for laborers. While unions might succeed in obtaining wage increases for their workers, they employ other practices—such as limiting labor—that result in decreased productivity. This affects prices of goods, which in turn minimizes laborers' real wages. George Reisman, Ph.D., is Pepperdine University Professor Emeritus of Economics and the author of Capitalism: A Treatise on Economics.

As you read, consider the following questions:

1. What is the only thing that explains a rise in real wages throughout an economic system, according to the author?
2. Why do unions seek to reduce the supply of labor?
3. What effect does countering the rise of productivity have on real wages?

"How Labor Unions Hurt Workers," by George Reisman, Mises Institute, September 7, 2014. Reprinted by permission.

Many Americans, perhaps a substantial majority, still believe that, irrespective of any problems they may have caused, labor unions are fundamentally an institution that exists in the vital self-interest of wage earners. Indeed, many believe that it is labor unions that stand between the average wage earner and a life of subsistence wages, exhausting hours of work, and horrific working conditions.

Labor unions and the general public almost totally ignore the essential role played by falling prices in achieving rising real wages. They see only the rise in money wages as worthy of consideration. Indeed, in our environment of chronic inflation, prices that actually do fall are relatively rare.

Nevertheless, the only thing that can explain a rise in real wages throughout the economic system is a fall in prices relative to wages. And the only thing that achieves this is an increase in production per worker. More production per worker—a higher productivity of labor—serves to increase the supply of goods and services produced relative to the supply of labor that produces them. In this way, it reduces prices relative to wages and thereby raises real wages and the general standard of living.

What raises money wages throughout the economic system is not what is responsible for the rise in real wages. Increases in money wages are essentially the result just of the increase in the quantity of money and resulting increase in the overall volume of spending in the economic system. In the absence of a rising productivity of labor, the increase in money and spending would operate to raise prices by as much or more than it raised wages. This outcome is prevented only by the fact that at the same time that the quantity of money and volume of spending are increasing, the output per worker is also increasing, with the result that prices rise by less than wages. A fall in prices is still present in the form of prices being lower than they would have been had only an increase in the quantity of money and volume of spending been operative.

With relatively minor exceptions, real wages throughout the economic system simply do not rise from the side of higher money wages. Essentially, they rise only from the side of a greater supply of goods and services relative to the supply of labor and thus from prices being lower relative to wages. The truth is that the means by which the standard of living of the individual wage earner and the individual businessman and capitalist is increased, and the means by which that of the average wage earner in the economic system is increased, are very different. For the individual, it is the earning of more money. For the average wage earner in the economic system, it is the payment of lower prices.

What this discussion shows is that the increase in money wages that labor unions seek is not at all the source of rising real wages and that the source of rising real wages is in fact a rising productivity of labor, which always operates from the side of falling prices, not rising money wages.

Indeed, the efforts of labor unions to raise money wages are profoundly opposed to the goal of raising real wages and the standard of living. When the unions seek to raise the standard of living of their members by means of raising their money wages, their policy inevitably comes down to an attempt to make the labor of their members artificially scarce. That is their only means of raising the wages of their members. The unions do not have much actual power over the demand for labor. But they often achieve considerable power over the supply of labor. And their actual technique for raising wages is to make the supply of labor, at least in the particular industry or occupation that a given union is concerned with, as scarce as possible.

Thus, whenever they can, unions attempt to gain control over entry into the labor market. They seek to impose apprenticeship programs, or to have licensing requirements imposed by the government. Such measures are for the purpose of holding down the supply of labor in the field and thereby enabling those fortunate enough to be admitted to it, to earn higher incomes. Even when the unions do not succeed in directly reducing the supply of labor, the imposition of their above-market wage demands still has the effect of reducing the number of jobs offered in the field and thus the supply of labor in the field that is able to find work.

The artificial wage increases imposed by the labor unions result in unemployment when above-market wages are imposed throughout the economic system. This situation exists when it is possible for unions to be formed easily. If, as in the present-day United States, all that is required is for a majority of workers in an establishment to decide that they wish to be represented by a union, then the wages imposed by the unions will be effective even in the nonunion fields.

Employers in the nonunion fields will feel compelled to offer their workers wages comparable to what the union workers are receiving—indeed, possibly even still higher wages—in order to ensure that they do not unionize.

Widespread wage increases closing large numbers of workers out of numerous occupations put extreme pressure on the wage rates of whatever areas of the economic system may still remain open. These limited areas could absorb the overflow of workers from other lines at low enough wage rates. But minimum-wage laws prevent wage rates in these remaining lines from going low enough to absorb these workers.

From the perspective of most of those lucky enough to keep their jobs, the most serious consequence of the unions is the holding down or outright reduction of the productivity of labor. With few exceptions, the labor unions openly combat the rise in the productivity of labor. They do so virtually as a matter of principle. They oppose the introduction of labor-saving machinery on the grounds that it causes unemployment. They oppose competition among workers. As Henry Hazlitt pointed out, they force employers to tolerate featherbedding practices, such as the classic requirement that firemen, whose function was to shovel coal on steam locomotives, be retained on diesel locomotives. They impose make-work schemes, such as requiring that pipe delivered to construction sites with screw thread already on it, have its ends cut off and new screw thread cut on the site. They impose narrow work classifications, and require that specialists be employed at a day's pay to perform work that others could easily do—for example, requiring the employment of a plasterer to repair the incidental damage done to a wall by an electrician, which the electrician himself could easily repair.

To anyone who understands the role of the productivity of labor in raising real wages, it should be obvious that the unions' policy of combating the rise in the productivity of labor renders them in fact a leading enemy of the rise in real wages. However radical this conclusion may seem, however much at odds it is with the prevailing view of the unions as the leading source of the rise in real wages over the last hundred and fifty years or more, the fact is that in combating the rise in the productivity of labor, the unions actively combat the rise in real wages!

Far from being responsible for improvements in the standard of living of the average worker, labor unions operate in more or less total ignorance of what actually raises the average worker's standard of living. In consequence of their ignorance, they are responsible for artificial inequalities in wage rates, for unemployment, and for holding down real wages and the average worker's standard of living. All of these destructive, antisocial consequences derive from the fact that while individuals increase the money they earn through increasing production and the overall supply of goods and services, thereby reducing prices and raising real wages throughout the economic system, labor unions increase the money paid to their members by exactly the opposite means. They reduce the supply and productivity of labor and so reduce the supply and raise the prices of the goods and services their members help to produce, thereby reducing real wages throughout the economic system.

| "*Employers can fire people for no reason. We shouldn't underestimate the degree people are fearful about what the employers say.*"

Big Companies Have the Power to Prevent Workers from Forming Unions

Ucilia Wang

Several previous viewpoints have referenced attempts by businesses to intimidate workers from forming unions. In the following viewpoint, Ucilia Wang discusses several such cases. The author argues that large corporations are in a position to easily threaten workers who attempt to organize, without necessarily breaking laws. This is a problem, she points out, because companies are at their most productive when workers have a voice. As she argues, corporate social responsibility includes investing in the well being of employees. In addition, Americans no longer have a more favorable view of unions as compared to corporations. Ucilia Wang is an American journalist and editor.

"Why Target's Anti-Union Video Is No Joke," by Ucilia Wang, Guardian News & Media Limited, March 31, 2014. Reprinted by permission.

As you read, consider the following questions:

1. Wang cites data showing that Americans' views of both unions and corporations dip when the economy is weak. Why might that be the case?
2. Why is it easier for large corporations to repress union activity, according to the viewpoint?
3. Why did unionization of the Volkswagen plant in Tennessee fail, despite Volkswagen's support of unionization?

E ven as the debate over raising the minimum wage gains public attention and the disparity between the rich and poor continues to grow, US membership in unions has continued what Philip Jennings, general secretary for UNI Global Union, calls "an alarming plunge," hitting a 97-year low last year.

The recent leak of Target's latest anti-union video highlights how effective corporate campaigns have been in undermining unionization efforts. It isn't the first anti-union video from Target: Gawker also posted a heavily panned video back in 2011, when the United Food and Commercial Workers International Union (UFCW) were attempting to unionize Target employees in Valley Stream, New York.

Had UFCW succeeded, that store would've become the first union shop among Target's 1,750 stores. UFCW told Salon, which first wrote about the most recent video, that it wasn't planning to seek another vote from Target employees to unionize.

It's easy to make fun of both videos for the characters' performance, the script or special effects. But the quality of the videos is beside the point, said John Logan, an associate professor in the San Francisco State University's labor and employment studies department. Both videos present essentially the same talking points, and the main message is this: Job security is at stake if you unionize because a union will undermine Target's competitiveness in a cutthroat business.

"If you see the video in isolation, it seems comical. But in the context of power dynamics that exist in the workplace, these statements are quite effective at dissuading employees," Logan said. "Employers can fire people for no reason. We shouldn't underestimate the degree people are fearful about what the employers say."

Corporate social responsibility includes the proper treatment of workers. That invariably affects a company's fortunes in the long run. The most shocking stories—and the ones that embarrass a company enough to force change—seem to come mostly from exposés about overseas factories, however. Think of Apple's attempt to address stories of workers' abuse at the giant campus of its supplier, Foxconn, in China.

What's happening elsewhere in the world—the terribly unsafe working conditions, paltry wages and ungodly long working hours —also used to exist in the United States. Those conditions gave rise to stronger labor protection laws at federal and state levels during the last century, when unions' influence also rose. Gallup polls in 1937 found that 72% of those surveyed approved of unions.

In recent years, however, Americans by and large no longer view unions any more favorably than they view businesses. In fact, their opinions tend to dip for both when the economy turns sour and go back up when the economy improves, according to Pew Research Center surveys.

Unions' power has fallen considerably in the past few decades. Changes in federal and state laws have made it more difficult to organize unions, and penalties against companies that illegally interfere with unionization campaigns aren't serious deterrents, especially for large companies with resources to fight. Gallup polls found the approval rating for unions dropped to 48% in 2009.

Union membership also has fallen from about 20% in 1983 to 11% in 2013, according to the US Bureau of Labor Statistics. About 35% of the public-sector workers belonged to a union in 2013, compared with only roughly 7% for private-sector employees.

Unionized workers on average make 30% higher wages and benefits than non-union workers, said Kent Wong, director of the Center for Labor Research and Education at the University of California at Los Angeles.

"There's tremendous incentives for corporations to intimidate the workers from joining the unions," Wong said.

Anti-union messages don't have to come from companies to be effective. The failed unionization effort by the United Auto Workers at a Volkswagen plant in Tennessee last month serves as an example. The German automaker was actually open to having the union at its plant. But Republican lawmakers campaigned against it and threatened to withhold tax incentives.

Could the public sentiment towards unions change? In recent years, the public has paid more attention to the rising disparity of incomes between the rich and the poor.

The Occupy Wall Street movement in 2011 and its slogan of "We are the 99%" highlighted the huge economic inequality. Edward Wolff of New York University found that the richest fifth of US families control about 89% of the country's wealth.

While the public attention is welcome, it won't likely translate into changes in labor laws that favor unions, said Kathy M. Newman, an English professor at Carnegie Mellon University who is writing a book about labor, media and culture in the 1950s.

"I think American business was at its most productive and powerful at the time when there was a high percentage of unionized workers," Newman said. "When workers have a democratic voice and given an avenue for their ideas to be heard, the companies perform better."

Target responded to multiple requests for comment about the latest video with the following line: "We communicate with our team members through a variety of channels, including videos."

Periodical and Internet Sources Bibliography

The following articles have been selected to supplement the diverse views presented in this chapter.

Eillie Anzilotti, "The Economy Is Booming, Your Salary Is Not: Blame the Decline of Unions," FastCompany, August 29, 2018. https://www.fastcompany.com/90227665/the-economy-is-booming-your-salary-is-not-blame-the-decline-of-unions.

Chris Brooks, "As Tenn. Workers Gear Up for Another Union Campaign, Local Media Shows Anti-Union Bias," In These Times, April 15, 2019. http://inthesetimes.com/working/entry/21844/volkswagen_uaw_union_campaign_tennessee_media_chattanooga.

Michelle Chen, "Union Benefits Go Far Beyond the Workplace," *Nation*, January 22, 2019. https://www.thenation.com/article/unions-labor-welfare.

Susan Dynarski, "Fresh Proof That Strong Unions Help Reduce Income Inequality," *New York Times*, July 6, 2018. https://www.nytimes.com/2018/07/06/business/labor-unions-income-inequality.html.

Rana Foroohar, "Strong Unions Will Boost America's Economy," *Financial Times*, July 31, 2017. https://www.ft.com/content/6965239a-6e30-11e7-bfeb-33fe0c5b7eaa.

Suresh Naidu, Eric Posner, and Glen Weyl, "More and More Companies Have Monopoly Power over Workers' Wages. That's Killing the Economy," Vox, April 6, 2018. https://www.vox.com/the-big-idea/2018/4/6/17204808/wages-employers-workers-monopsony-growth-stagnation-inequality.

Jonathan Rauch, "The Conservative Case for Unions," *Atlantic*, July/August 2017. https://www.theatlantic.com/magazine/archive/2017/07/the-conservative-case-for-unions/528708.

Noam Scheiber, "Labor's Hard Choice in Amazon Age: Play Along or Get Tough," *New York Times*, February 22, 2019. https://www.nytimes.com/2019/02/22/business/economy/labor-unions-amazon.html.

OPPOSING
VIEWPOINTS®
SERIES

CHAPTER 3

Do Unions Contribute to Political Corruption?

Chapter Preface

One of the recurring criticisms of unions is that they tend to be corrupt or foster corruption in their leaders. Popular movies of a certain time, such as *Norma Rae* and *Harlan County, USA*, often depict union organizers sympathetically. Yet the stereotype of the cigar-chewing union boss embezzling dues, taking kickbacks, and cutting deals with management has been difficult for organized labor to shake.

And indeed, there has been some serious corruption in American unions over the years. The Teamsters have an especially unsavory history. (The official name of the Teamsters union is The International Brotherhood of Teamsters and it represents workers in many industries.) For example, in Kansas City in the first half of the twentieth century, Teamsters officials went as far as extortion and even violence to gain control over the trucking and construction industries there. Organized crime has often infiltrated unions. Again, the Teamsters are among the best-known examples of mob infiltration of unions.

In the late 1950s, a Congressional committee known as the McClellan Committee investigated and found widespread corruption in the Teamsters. The committee even uncovered a plot to seize control of the Oregon state government through blackmail and bribery. (The Teamsters weren't the only unions to be caught up in corruption, but they were the most widely-known for it.)

In the end, however, it was not the government that cleared out the corrupt leadership, but the unions themselves. The AFL-CIO, an organization that is a federation of many individual unions, fearing that the government would dilute or even remove legal protections for unions, took strong measure to bring its member unions in line. In the early 1990s, rank and file Teamsters members rose up to vote out the corrupt leadership and elect a better crop of leaders. Today there are still cases of corrupt union officials, but the problems are no longer as egregious and widespread.

The viewpoints in this chapter examine the issues of corruption in organized labor, however not all from the obvious perspective. Some simply point out the temptations of money and power offered by union leadership. Others focus on political corruption that takes aim at workers' rights.

> "When it is difficult for workers to reject or replace a union, there is an immense temptation for union officials to sit back and enjoy the dues payments—or stand up and steal from the pension fund."

Laws That Protect Unions Encourage Corruption

Robert VerBruggen

In the following viewpoint, Robert VerBruggen explains how laws that were intended to strengthen unions have often had the effect of making them ripe for corruption. Organized crime, he says, has taken advantage of government protections for unions, corrupted union leaders, and taken advantage of the trust of union members. Right-to-work laws, he writes, are part of the solution, in that they would allow workers to not pay union dues. Robert VerBruggen is deputy managing editor of National Review.

"Organized Labor, Organized Crime," by Robert VerBruggen, *National Review*, January 24, 2011. Reprinted by permission.

As you read, consider the following questions:

1. How do current laws facilitate union corruption?
2. Does VerBruggen believe that right-to-work laws would rein in corruption in unions?
3. How would transparency laws reduce corruption in unions, according to this viewpoint?

With its arrest of more than 100 alleged mobsters in New York, New Jersey, and Rhode Island on Thursday, the FBI made it crystal clear that the Mafia, while a shadow of its former self, is still a significant force in much of the country. The grand-jury indictments—which read like a *Sopranos* episode, with nicknames like "Lumpy" and strip clubs called the Satin Doll and the Cadillac Lounge—accuse the arrestees of crimes ranging from murder to selling untaxed cigarettes, going back several decades.

And just as organized crime hasn't disappeared since the days of *On the Waterfront*, organized labor hasn't managed to sever its ties with the Mafia. The indictments allege that the mob corrupted Cement and Concrete Workers Union Local 6A (which is headquartered in Flushing, Queens), taking from its honest members "labor union positions, money paid as wages and other economic benefits," as well as the right "to free speech and [a] democratic process in the affairs of their labor organization." Named in the indictments is Ralph Scopo Jr., a former head of the union. His father ran the organization's district council and was convicted of racketeering in the 1980s, and his son (who was not indicted) runs the union now.

Also among those indicted are Albert Cernadas Sr., who stepped down five years ago as executive vice president of the International Longshoreman's Association and head of ILA Local 1235, as well as the son of the man who replaced him at 1235, Edward Aulisi—prosecutors say Aulisi was recorded promising continued payments to the mob after Cernadas left. The current president of 1235, Thomas Leonardis, was indicted, as was Nunzio LaGrasso, vice president of ILA Local 1478.

Union corruption is only one part of what the Mafia does. But it's important to recognize that our laws facilitate it, as I detailed in *Labor Watch* at length last year—and as even some pro-labor leftists have acknowledged.

Unions' power comes from the federal government's guarantee of monopoly bargaining—that is, when a workplace elects a union, the union has the right to negotiate for all the employees, including the ones who voted against it or would rather negotiate with the employer directly. In the 22 states with right-to-work laws, workers can protest by refusing to join the union or pay dues, though they are still bound by the union contract. By contrast, non-right-to-work states—which include New York, New Jersey, and Rhode Island—reason that it is unfair to allow workers to free-ride on union efforts this way. So, they permit "union shop" agreements, which make dues payments a condition of employment after a certain period of time.

In addition, it is quite difficult to get rid of an existing union, or even to replace it with a competing one. This creates a situation in which the organization is guaranteed a consistent cash flow no matter what it does. Adding to the cash is the fact that unions often handle pension and benefits funds—despite evidence that employers do a better job at that task.

These laws were passed with the intention of strengthening unions, but as liberal journalist Robert Fitch argues in his excellent book *Solidarity for Sale*, they may have weakened unions by engendering corruption and laziness. When it is difficult for workers to reject or replace a union, there is an immense temptation for union officials to sit back and enjoy the dues payments—or stand up and steal from the pension fund. Some of Fitch's proposed solutions sound like an American conservative's dream—he would end monopoly bargaining and the union shop, for example. (Others, not so much: He would forbid employers to resist unions or hire replacements when workers strike, and would form "works councils" that give employees a say in how business owners run their companies.)

Of course, union corruption is already illegal, and as we saw with Thursday's bust, law enforcement isn't ignoring the problem. Sometimes, unions are even put under RICO trusteeships—that is, under the Racketeer Influenced and Corrupt Organizations Act, the federal government takes them over temporarily to expel mob influence.

However, these trusteeships aren't particularly effective, and it's difficult for the government to monitor unions if little transparency is required of them. Of the 20 trusteeships that legal scholar and sociologist James B. Jacobs evaluated in *Mobsters, Unions, and Feds*, he found only seven to be qualified or clear successes. And while Bush 43's labor secretary, Elaine Chao, implemented rules forcing unions to disclose the names of anyone who received more than $5,000 in union funds, the Obama administration wasted no time in dismantling her progress.

Ideally, the federal government would end its legal guarantee that established unions can represent workers without their consent, or, at the very least, more states would enact right-to-work laws. But failing that, the Republican House should use the recent arrests as evidence that the current administration was wrong to roll back union transparency.

> "Strong unions have helped reduce inequality, whereas weaker unions have made it easier for CEOs, sometimes working with market forces that they have helped shape, to increase it."

Union Members Themselves Thwart Corruption

Alexia Fernández Campbell

In the previous viewpoint, the author argued that right-to-work laws would prevent corruption in unions. In the following viewpoint, Alexia Fernández Campbell argues that such laws would cripple unions. This viewpoint was written as a response to an unsuccessful attempt to pass right-to-work legislation in the state of Missouri. The author points out that it also was rank and file union members who defeated the legislation, not merely corrupt union leaders. Alexia Fernández Campbell is a journalist who covers economic policy for Vox Media.

"Missouri Voters Just Blocked the Right-to-Work Law Republicans Passed to Weaken Labor Union," by Alexia Fernández Campbell, Vox Media, Inc, February 2, 2012. Reprinted by permission.

As you read, consider the following questions:

1. What argument did the Missouri governor make in support of right-to-work legislation?
2. Why, according to this viewpoint, is right-to-work legislation anti-union?
3. Does the author imply that the interference with unions by Republican leaders, big businesses, and the courts in order to enrich corporate leaders is itself a type of corruption?

Missouri voters made history on Tuesday, blocking the state's Republican lawmakers from enacting right-to-work laws to cripple labor unions. The state's primary voters rejected Proposition A, which would have made it illegal for unions to charge fees to workers they represent who don't want to pay them, by a two-to-one margin when the vote was called by Decision Desk around 10 pm Eastern.

Missouri was on track to become the 28th state to enact such a law. Last year, the state's then-governor, Republican Eric Greitens, signed the right-to-work bill, saying that it would encourage businesses to move to the state. Missouri would have followed Michigan, Wisconsin, and other Rust Belt states that have passed similar anti-union measures in recent years under pressure from business groups.

But workers and union leaders in Missouri put up a fight. They gathered about 300,000 signatures—more than double the number needed—to freeze the law and put it on the ballot for voters to decide. On Tuesday, voters rejected the bill.

Tuesday's election marks the first time voters have overturned a right-to-work law through a ballot referendum since Ohio did something similar in 2011. No other state has even tried to in recent years. It's also a major victory for the US labor movement at a time when Republican leaders, big businesses, and the courts have doubled down on their attempts to weaken the influence of labor unions and the workers they represent. And after the US Supreme Court's June ruling in *Janus v. AFSCME*, which mandated right-to-work rules for all government unions, Missouri's vote is a sign that unions are far from dead. They might even see a revival.

Workers Have Been Waging a War in Missouri to Defeat the Law

In states without right-to-work laws, employees at unionized workplaces don't have to pay union dues, but they do have to pay "agency fees." These fees are lower than the dues members pay, but they cover the union's cost of negotiating employment contracts that benefit all workers. Right-to-work laws make it illegal for a union to charge those fees, which can strain its finances and give workers an incentive not to pay dues. This is known as the "free rider" problem, in which some workers benefit from union contracts but choose not to pay for it.

That's what Missouri politicians wanted.

But workers and unions in Missouri have fought back. They built a massive campaign to defeat the Republican law, gathering 300,000 signatures to put the referendum on the ballot. Construction workers, ironworkers, and steelworkers knocked on about half a million doors to mobilize voters to the polls, according to the AFL-CIO, the nation's largest federation of unions. A union-backed group raised $15 million for the effort—more than five times the amount of money raised by two business groups supporting the right-to-work bill.

Labor groups had framed the issue as a fight between workers and greedy billionaires. The campaign even enlisted actor John Goodman, a Missouri native, for a 30-second radio ad.

"The bill will not give you the right to work," Goodman says in the spot. "It's being sold as a way to help Missouri workers, but look a little deeper and you'll see it's all about corporate greed."

That message has resonated with unionized workers across the country, whose wages remain flat as CEOs earn record-high salaries and corporations reap massive tax cuts.

Teachers across the country have led the revolt against such pro-business policies that swept through conservative states in the past decade—policies that never led to the promised economic boom. With the support of their labor unions, teachers in states like Arizona, Oklahoma, and West Virginia have forced state lawmakers to raise business taxes to pay better wages.

Missouri might be the start of a similar backlash, one targeted toward Republican right-to-work policies that hurt labor unions and the middle-class workers they represent.

Right-to-Work Laws Are Great for Businesses, Not Workers

When Republicans took over a historic number of state legislatures in the 2010 midterms, they focused on two things: cutting taxes and weakening labor unions. With support from pro-business groups, lawmakers began to expand right-to-work laws from the South to Midwestern states with a strong union presence.

In 2012, lawmakers in Indiana and Michigan passed these laws. At the time, the country was in the midst of the Great Recession, and politicians promised that relaxing labor laws would attract businesses to the state and turn around the economy. Since then, Wisconsin, Kentucky, and West Virginia have passed right-to-work laws too.

Economists have been closely studying the economic impact, and none have found any evidence to back up the claim that right-to-work laws boost the economy. At best, the laws slightly increase the number of businesses in the state, but they don't really benefit workers. At worst, these laws lower average wages for all workers after they are passed. The latter is the most likely outcome, based on the research.

One study conducted by economist Lonnie Stevans at Hofstra University in 2007 found that right-to-work laws did lead to an increase in the number of businesses, but those economic gains mostly went to business owners. Meanwhile, average wages for workers went down.

International Examples Show Only Strong Unions Defeat Corruption

Detailed Australian research demonstrates that corrupt practices within unions are best defeated from within unions, rather than subjecting unions to criminalisation and oppressive regulation by the state.

This research reveals that only strong unions tend to defeat corruption. Strong unions are those that are able to foster internal cultures of democracy through networks of membership participation and communication, as free as possible from interference by a hostile media and political arena.

Indeed, the historical experience of union-busting in the United States provides clear evidence that regulation leads to weakness, desperation and further corruption within unions.

Almost every comparable advanced economy to Australia (including Britain, Sweden, Denmark and Germany) maintains strong codes of corporate regulation. Unions are not regulated by the State, and in many cases are protected by constitutional rights to collectively bargain, as well as the freedom of association (for instance the United States).

"Strikes Are Good for Us All," by Eugene Schofield-Georgeson, the Conversation, 01/08/2016. https://theconversation.com/corporate-style-regulation-of-unions-wont-defeat-corruption-52759. Licensed under CC BY-ND 4.0 International.

One 2015 study showed that Oklahoma's right-to-work law didn't lead to more jobs, but it also didn't seem to affect wages.

The Economic Policy Institute, a left-leaning think tank, attributes right-to-work laws to a 3.1 percent decline in wages for union and nonunion workers after accounting for differences in cost of living, demographics, and labor market characteristics.

Had voters in Missouri approved Proposition A, they would probably see a similar drop in income, according to economists at the University of Missouri Kansas City. In a 2014 study, they concluded that Missouri's shifting to a right-to-work state would result in an annual loss of $1,945 to $2,547 per household.

It shouldn't be a surprise that anti-union laws would hurt middle-class families. The decline of labor unions is largely responsible for the growing income inequality in the United States.

Missouri Could Reverse The Decline

Back in the 1950s, about one-third of American workers belonged to labor unions. Today, only about one in 10 workers are unionized.

Vox's Dylan Matthew explains why this happened:

> This is the culmination of decades of decline in private sector unions in America, caused by a variety of factors including slower employment growth in unionized workplaces (compared to nonunion workplaces); anti-union legislation, particularly in the South and more recently the Midwest; the automation, offshoring, and general decline of union-heavy industries like textiles and auto manufacturing; and more sophisticated corporate anti-union drives.

Labor unions were largely credited with helping maintain stable middle-class factory jobs in Rust Belt states like Missouri in the '50s and '60s. But the disappearance of manufacturing jobs, plus the aggressive corporate lobbying to weaken labor unions, has been a driving force behind the massive income gap in the United States.

In 1965, CEOs earned an average salary that was 20 times higher than the average worker's; by 2016, their salaries were 271 times higher.

Nobel Prize–winning economist Joseph Stiglitz described the dynamic this way:

> Strong unions have helped reduce inequality, whereas weaker unions have made it easier for CEOs, sometimes working with market forces that they have helped shape, to increase it. The decline in unionization since World War II in the United States has been associated with a pronounced rise in income and wealth inequality.

Missouri voters—and workers across the country—have shown that they are ready to reverse that trend.

> *"This is yet another case where the government is working for a tiny elite against the interests of the bulk of the population."*

Corruption Is Not Limited to the Mob

Dean Baker

Unions have traditionally been opposed to free trade agreements and typically support more protectionist policies in the belief that those policies protect American jobs. In the following viewpoint, Dean Baker points out that the difference between free trade and protectionism is not always clear—and corruption is not always limited to the mob. This viewpoint was written during the time the US was debating two additional free trade deals. Dean Baker, economist and cofounder of the Center for Economic Policy Research, says here that both agreements were less about free trade than improving regulatory conditions for large corporations.

"Political Corruption and the 'Free Trade' Racket," by Dean Baker, Al Jazeera Media Network, April 29, 2013. Reprinted by permission.

As you read, consider the following questions:

1. Why are policies regarding copyright and intellectual property more important in the current economy than policies regarding imports of physical items such as steel?
2. Why, according to the author, will members of Congress feel so much pressure to support these trade agreements?
3. Does the political power of giant corporations, with their ability to make large campaign donations to Congress members, negate the power of unions?

In polite circles in the United States, support for free trade is a bit like proper bathing habits: It is taken for granted. Only the hopelessly crude and unwashed would not support free trade.

There is some ground for this attitude. Certainly, the US has benefited enormously by being able to buy a wide range of items at lower cost from other countries. However, this does not mean that most people in the country have always benefited from every opening to greater trade.

And it certainly does not mean that the country will benefit from everything that those in power label as "free trade." That is the story we are seeing now as the Obama administration is pursuing two major "free trade" agreements that in fact have very little to do with free trade and are likely to hurt those without the money and power to be part of the game.

The deals in questions, the Trans-Pacific Partnership (TPP) and the US-European Union "Free Trade" Agreement are both being pushed as major openings to trade that will increase growth and create jobs. In fact, eliminating trade restrictions is a relatively small part of both agreements, since most tariffs and quotas have already been sharply reduced or eliminated.

Rather, these deals are about securing regulatory gains for major corporate interests. In some cases, such as increased patent and copyright protection, these deals are 180 degrees at odds with free trade. They are about increasing protectionist barriers.

All the arguments that trade economists make against tariffs and quotas apply to patent and copyright protection. The main difference is the order of magnitude. Tariffs and quotas might raise the price of various items by 20 or 30 percent. By contrast, patent and copyright protection is likely to raise the price of protected items 2,000 percent or even 20,000 percent above the free market price. Drugs that would sell for a few dollars per prescription in a free market would sell for hundreds or even thousands of dollars when the government gives a drug company a patent monopoly.

In the case of drug patents, the costs go beyond just dollars and cents. Higher drug prices will have a direct impact on the public's health, especially in some of the poorer countries that might end up being parties to these agreements.

There are also a wide variety of regulatory issues that are being pursued through these agreements in large part because there would be difficulty getting them accepted through the normal political process. For example, the sort of government mandated internet policing that was part of the shipwrecked Stop Online Piracy Act is likely to reappear in one or both agreements.

It is also likely that rules that limit the power of governments to restrict fracking could be in the agreements. Such rules could prohibit not only the federal government, but also state or county governments, from imposing restrictions designed to protect the public's health.

These are the sorts of restrictions that may appear in the TPP and US-EU Free Trade Agreement. The reason for using tentative language is that none of the specifics of the deal have yet been made public. The Obama administration is negotiating these pacts in secret. It has made almost nothing about the negotiating process public and has shared none of the proposed text with the relevant committees in Congress (Public Citizen has posted information on the TPP based on leaked documents).

Incredibly, it has shared portions of the proposed TPP with the relevant industry groups. While elected representatives in Congress may not be able to find out anything about proposed rules on drug patents or restrictions on fracking, Pfizer and Merck will have the opportunity to weigh in on patent rules and the major oil and gas companies will help to draft language on fracking that serves their interests.

The idea is that once a deal is completed there will be enormous political pressure for Congress to approve it no matter what it contains. In addition to the campaign contributions that supporters of the deals will get from the special interest groups who stand to benefit, news outlets like the *Washington Post* will use both their news and opinion sections to bash members of Congress who oppose a deal. They will be endlessly portrayed as ignorant Neanderthals who do not understand economics.

The reality of course is that it is the "free traders" who either do not understand economics or deliberately choose to ignore it. Many of the provisions that we are likely to see in these deals, like stronger patent protections, will slow growth and cost jobs.

These deals will also lead to more upward redistribution of income. The more money that people in the developing world pay to Pfizer for drugs and Microsoft for software, the less money they will pay for the products that we export, as opposed to "intellectual property rights." These payments are great if you own lots of stock in drug or software companies, but for the vast majority of the nation's workers who are not big stockholders, extracting money from people in the developing world for these corporate giants is not good news.

This is yet another case where the government is working for a tiny elite against the interests of the bulk of the population. And it is doing it in a way that would be difficult to caricature: making powerful corporate interests direct negotiating partners, while excluding democratically elected representatives from the process.

It is tempting to say that Washington could not get more corrupt, but it probably will.

"In all but the most superficial respects, corporations and labor unions are virtually identical to each other."

Government Corrupts the Purpose of Both Unions and Corporations

Tom Mullen

In some of the previous viewpoints, authors have suggested that the interests of unions and the interests of large corporations were fundamentally opposed. In the following viewpoint, Tom Mullen turns that assumption on its head. He argues that unions and corporations are pretty much identical—and the corruption resides in neither unions nor corporations, but the government. However, his view of what amounts to "corruption" is a bit different from those of previous authors. Tom Mullen is the author of A Return to Common Sense: Reawakening Liberty in the Inhabitants of America.

"Corporations and Labor Unions: Great Ideas Corrupted by Government," by Tom Mullen, Tom Mullen/ Genesis Framework, March 4, 2019. Reprinted by permission.

As you read, consider the following questions:

1. Why is the limitation of risk afforded by incorporation important to an economy?
2. How might that change if, as the author suggests, corporations were only protected from liability by those who voluntarily agreed to release them from responsibility?
3. How does the National Labor Relations Act and simlar legislation violate the rights of employers according to the viewpoint?

There are no two institutions in American society more associated with the struggle between right and left than corporations and labor unions. Outside of foreign policy, there is nothing liberals are more hostile towards than corporations, nor anything conservatives are more hostile towards than labor unions. For most Americans, corporations and labor unions lie at opposite ends of the socio-economic spectrum. Corporations are "conservative and capitalist," while labor unions are "liberal and socialist."

This is an illusion. In all but the most superficial respects, corporations and labor unions are virtually identical to each other. They are both voluntary associations formed by individuals to achieve an economic goal. They would both provide enormous economic benefits to society if they were not completely corrupted by government.

A corporation is a group of people agreeing to pool their capital to create a larger venture than any of them could launch individually. The stockholders agree that none of their personal assets will be put at risk if the venture fails—only the assets of the corporation.

The stockholders also make these terms with the corporation's creditors, customers, and other parties. In this way, the stockholders can cooperatively take more risk than they would if their personal assets were at stake. With greater risk comes greater reward. Thus corporations are able to innovate, produce, and expand more rapidly than smaller partnerships or sole-owner proprietorships. This benefits consumers by offering them more choice and higher quality products at lower prices.

The benefits of corporations are derived from the voluntary nature of every transaction. The stockholders, creditors, and customers all consent to doing business with the corporation, knowing the risks and the limited liability of the stockholders. All parties are exercising a natural right to associate and exchange their property as they see fit. One can never harm another merely by exercising one's natural rights.

The prospect of the corporation becoming "too large" or dominant in a particular industry is countered by the equal right of all other members of society to form their own corporations and compete with the dominant one. In fact, it is this natural market occurrence—new competitors entering the market when there is an opportunity to offer consumers the same or better products at lower prices—that drives explosive innovation and growth and confers enormous benefits on the rest of society.

All of the associations necessary to realize these benefits can be achieved by voluntary contract. There is no reason that a government must enact a body of laws indicating how these corporations should be formed or how they should operate. Neither is there any reason why the government must create an "artificial legal person" in order to insulate stockholders from liability. That can be achieved by voluntary contract as well. All that is necessary is that the various contracts made between parties be enforced. However, voluntary association is not the government's purpose in enacting corporate laws.[1]

The government corrupts the entire nature of corporations in virtually every way. First, it grants the corporation limited liability that applies not only to those who have consented to it, but to everyone. This completely skews a natural risk/reward balance and enables the corporation to commit torts against third parties without consequences to the stockholders. It overrides the right of individuals who did not voluntarily release the corporation from liability to pursue compensation for damages. It also has the effect of encouraging corporations to take more risk than they would if the stockholders' personal assets were at risk with respect to these third parties.

Second, the enormous body of regulations constructed around corporations harms both the stockholders and the rest of society. The stockholders have the right to form and operate their corporation any way they see fit, as long as they do not invade the life or property of non-contracted parties. Regulations override their decisions and force them to operate the way the government tells them to, regardless of whether it is the best way or not. This adds tremendous costs to operating the corporation, which is then passed on to consumers.

Worst of all, these unnaturally high operating costs create impediments to the rest of society in exercising its most important right in this area: to form new corporations and compete with existing firms. This inevitably results in a few companies dominating each sector of the economy. Not only are consumers punished with higher prices and less choice than they could expect in a free market, but when these government-protected corporations get into financial trouble, those same consumers are often punished again when the government bails the corporations out with taxpayer funds. Without easy entry into the market for competitors, any corporation providing a service for which there is high demand becomes "too big to fail."

Thanks to the corrupting hand of government, corporations are motivated to do exactly the opposite of what they would do if that artificial force were absent. Instead of trying to produce better products at lower prices, the corporation has an incentive to lobby the government for higher tariffs which keep out foreign competition. This allows them to keep operating inefficiently and charging higher prices than they could if they had to compete with the true market prices offered by those competing firms.

They also benefit by lobbying for more regulations that drive up their own operating costs. Why would they do something so illogical? They do it because those higher costs provide an entry barrier to new competitors. The established firm can pass those higher costs on to consumers, while the new competitor is either unable to start-up at all or unable to compete until it can match the established firms' economies of scale. In the long run, government involvement with corporations results in lower quality, higher prices, and less choice for consumers than would occur in a free market.

The dynamics at play in regard to labor unions are virtually identical. Just like the stockholders of a corporation, the members of a labor union are exercising a natural right to enter into agreements with each other in order to achieve results that they would not be able to achieve individually. They form a partnership wherein all members agree not to accept compensation below a certain agreed upon amount. Compensation can take the form of any combination of wages, benefits, or working conditions.

It is important to recognize that the relationship between employee and employer is a buyer/seller relationship, with the employer being the buyer who purchases services from the employee. Like all buyer/seller relationships, both parties benefit when the transaction is voluntary. The seller benefits by getting the very highest price for his product that the market will bear. The buyer benefits by getting the highest quality product that he is able to obtain for the money he is willing and able to spend. If either party in any buyer/seller transaction does not believe that he is benefitting from the transaction, he can refuse to go through with it.

In the case of labor unions and employers, the union members benefit by higher compensation for their services. By bargaining collectively, they can control the supply of a particular type of labor demanded by employers and thus drive up the price. However, the employers actually benefit as well. As they are free to choose to hire people outside the union, the union must ensure that their product (labor) is superior enough in quality to persuade the employer to pay more for union employees than for cheaper, non-union employees. Such are the incentives in a free market, where all transactions are voluntary.

Under these conditions, labor unions would have an incentive to offer continuing education or training courses, to monitor the productivity of their members, to set minimum standards for entry into the union and to establish criteria for expelling non-productive employees. All of this would drive up quality, productivity, and profitability, further encouraging employers to pay more for union employees as a wise investment in more profitable products.

As with corporations, the benefits conferred upon society by labor unions depends upon contracts being enforced and all transactions between parties being voluntary. However, just as it does with corporations, government completely corrupts the nature of labor unions, eliminating many of the benefits they would otherwise provide. With interventions like the National Labor Relations Act of 1935 and subsequent legislation, the government destroys the voluntary nature of the employment contract, in many cases forcing employers to hire union workers. This violates the rights of employers to purchase services from whomever they wish and eliminates competition for the labor unions, encouraging them to behave in a manner completely contrary to how they would behave in a free market.

Instead of encouraging their members to be more productive, labor unions actually encourage lower productivity from their members. It is not uncommon for a union member to be threatened by his coworkers for working too fast or being too productive and skewing the lower expectations negotiated by the union in the interest of employing more dues-paying members to accomplish the same work. Instead of setting higher standards for entry into the union, the union actually forces new employees to join as a condition of taking the job.

Finally, with competition from non-union employees eliminated, the union has no incentive to control the price they are charging for their services. In a free market, there would be a price point at which the presumably lower-skilled non-union workers would be a more profitable buy for employers than the presumably higher-skilled union workers. However, once the government removes the ability of the employer to make this choice, there is no longer any control on the price of union labor. This is why unions played such a large role in the demise of the American auto industry and American manufacturing in general.

Despite the unnatural, corruptive influence of government, corporations and labor unions still manage to provide many benefits to society. Often overlooked is that all of the benefits they provide derive from the extent to which they are voluntary associations entering into consensual agreements with other parties. Conversely, all of the harm they cause and all of the animosity they and their supporters have for each other are the result of the coercive interference of government.

Instead of appealing to the government to assist them in invading each other's rights, they should recognize that the government is their common enemy, preventing each from benefitting themselves and each other. If they wish to secure their rights and achieve positive results for themselves and society, they should kick the government out of their affairs and follow the law of nature.

Notes
1. Special thanks to libertarian thinker and activist Steve LaBianca for his help in developing this analysis of the nature of corporations.

Periodical and Internet Sources Bibliography

The following articles have been selected to supplement the diverse views presented in this chapter.

Daniel DiSalvo, "The Trouble with Public Sector Unions," *National Affairs,* Spring 2019. https://www.nationalaffairs.com/publications/detail/the -trouble-with-public-sector-unions.

Garrett Epps, "The Supreme Court Case That Could Clobber Public-Sector Unions," *Atlantic,* January 21, 2014. https://www.theatlantic.com /business/archive/2014/01/the-supreme-court-case-that-could-clobber -public-sector-unions/283232.

John Hinderaker. "Why Public Sector Unions Are Inherently Corrupt," Center of the American Experiment, March 1, 2018. https://www .americanexperiment.org/2018/03/public-sector-unions-inherently -corrupt.

Marick F. Masters, "Labor Must Fight the Perception of Corruption: Here's How," *Detroit Free Press*, January 14, 2018. https://www.freep.com /story/opinion/contributors/2018/01/14/labor-corruption/1026435001.

Eugene Methvin, "A Corrupt Union and the Mob," *Weekly Standard*, August 31, 1998. https://www.weeklystandard.com/eugene-h-methvin/a -corrupt-union-and-the-mob.

John Nichols, "Bernie Sanders Is Making Union Solidarity an Essential Theme of the 2020 Campaign," *Nation*, April 8, 2019. https://www .thenation.com/article/bernie-sanders-labor-union-speech-2020.

People's World, "How the Corporate Right Lies About Union Corruption," March 25, 2006. https://www.peoplesworld.org/article/how-the -corporate-right-lies-about-union-corruption.

Francis Rooney, "Strengthen Labor Union Reporting Requirements to Expose Corruption," *Hill*, March 18, 2019. https://thehill.com /blogs/congress-blog/labor/434617-strengthen-labor-union-reporting -requirements-to-expose-corruption.

Solidarity Center, "Unions Are Unique in Their Ability to Help End Corruption," May 17, 2016. https://www.solidaritycenter.org/unions -can-help-end-corruption.

Robert VerBruggen, "Unions on the Waterfront: Why Is Big Labor Prone to Corruption?" Capital Research Center, June 2010. https:// capitalresearch.org/article/unions-on-the-waterfront-why-is-big-labor -prone-to-corruption.

OPPOSING
VIEWPOINTS®
SERIES

CHAPTER 4

Does Right-to-Work Protection Harm Workers?

Chapter Preface

R ight-to-work legislation has been the focus of a tremendous amount of debate ever since 1947, when the Taft-Hartley Act made it illegal to force an employee to join a union, and therefore legal for states to pass laws making it illegal to force workers to pay union dues. This debate has grown even fiercer since the early twenty-first century, when many states began passing right-to-work laws.

Voters are understandably confused about these debates. Partly this is because the legislation is misleadingly named. Right-to-work legislation has nothing to do with the right to work; it has everything to do with the right to not pay union dues. Even beyond that, the question is not at all a simple one. On the one hand, it seems obvious to most voters that in a free society, people should not be forced to pay dues to an organization that they do not belong to.

On the other hand, it is just as clear—as one of the following viewpoints explains—that if the majority of the citizens in a democracy vote to create a system of taxes to pay for services, then all the citizens who live in that democracy and thus benefit from those services must be required to pay their share. If paying taxes were voluntary, then public services, such as roads, schools, and clean water, would soon be a thing of the past. In the same way, the argument goes, if a worker receives the benefits of union representation, then that worker should be expected to chip in for the cost of that representation. Meanwhile, supporters argue that workplaces are private not public, so different reasoning applies.

And if all that weren't confusing enough, the philosophical underpinnings of right-to-work supporters vary quite a bit. Some supporters are unexpectedly pro-business conservatives who feel that giving more power and benefits to corporations strengthens the economy. Others are libertarians who are likely to believe in a completely free market economy and equal freedom for the individuals in that economy.

> *"Right-to-work has nothing to do with people being forced to be union members."*

Right-to-Work: What It Is and What It Isn't

David Madland, Karla Walter, and Ross Eisenbrey

In the following viewpoint, David Madland, Karla Walter, and Ross Eisenbrey provide a succinct overview of what right-to-work laws actually are. Then they go on to explain why they believe such laws are damaging for unions, local economies, and the middle class in general. The authors counter several of the common arguments in support of these confusingly named laws. David Madland is a scholar specializing in economics and the author of Hollowed Out: Why the Economy Doesn't Work Without a Strong Middle Class, *published in 2015. Karla Walter is a research analyst and director of the American Worker Project at the Center for American Progress. Ross Eisenbrey is an expert on labor policy.*

"Right-to-Work 101," by David Madland, Karla Walter, and Ross Eisenbrey, Center for American Progress, February 2, 2012. Reprinted by permission.

As you read, consider the following questions:

1. How are right-to-work laws different from existing federal legislation that guarantees no one can be forced to join a union, according to this viewpoint?
2. In this viewpoint, the authors say that workplace injuries are higher in states with right-to-work laws. From what you've read so far, why do you think that might be the case?
3. What do the authors suggest may be the unstated reason some people support right-to-work laws?

In states where the law exists, "right-to-work" makes it illegal for workers and employers to negotiate a contract requiring everyone who benefits from a union contract to pay their fair share of the costs of administering it. Right-to-work has nothing to do with people being forced to be union members.

Federal law already guarantees that no one can be forced to be a member of a union, or to pay any amount of dues or fees to a political or social cause they don't support. What right-to-work laws do is allow some workers to receive a free ride, getting the advantages of a union contract—such as higher wages and benefits and protection against arbitrary discipline—without paying any fee associated with negotiating on these matters.

That's because the union must represent all workers with the same due diligence regardless of whether they join the union or pay it dues or other fees and a union contract must cover all workers, again regardless of their membership in or financial support for the union. In states without right-to-work laws, workers covered by a union contract can refuse union membership and pay a fee covering only the costs of workplace bargaining rather than the full cost of dues.

There is scant evidence these laws create jobs, help workers, or are good for a state's economy, as supporters claim. Instead, these laws weaken unions and thereby hurt workers, the middle class, and local economies. We present here a Right-to-Work 101 so that the debate over right-to-work laws proceeds based on the facts.

Right-to-Work Laws Don't Create Jobs

Researchers who study the impact of right-to-work laws find that these laws do not create jobs—despite supporters' claims to the contrary. The Indiana Chamber of Commerce, for example, claims that "unionization increases labor costs," and therefore makes a given location less attractive to capital. The purpose, then, of right-to-work laws is to undermine unions and therefore lower wages in a given state, thus attracting more companies into the state.

But in practice this low-road strategy for job creation just doesn't pan out. Despite boosters' promises of job creation, researchers find that right-to-work had "no significant positive impact whatsoever on employment" in Oklahoma, the only state to have adopted a right-to-work law over the past 25 years–until Indiana did so days ago–and consequently the best example of how a new adopter of right-to-work laws might fare in today's economy. In fact, both the number of companies relocating to Oklahoma and the total number of manufacturing jobs in the state fell by about a third since it adopted such a law in 2001.

Indeed, most right-to-work advocates' purported evidence of job growth is based on outdated research and misleading assertions. An Indiana Chamber of Commerce-commissioned study found right-to-work states had higher employment growth between 1977 and 2008 compared to states without a right-to-work law, but much of that growth could be attributed to other factors. Those factors included the states' infrastructure quality, and even its weather—which the study ignored.

Recent research from the Economic Policy Institute that controlled for these factors finds that right-to-work laws have not increased employment growth in the 22 states that have adopted them.

Right-to-Work Laws Hurt Workers

Right-to-work laws lower worker pay and benefits and make workplaces more dangerous for all workers—whether unionized or not—by weakening unions.

Unions have a significant and positive effect on the wages and benefits of union and nonunion workers alike. Unionized workers are able to bargain for better wages, benefits, and work conditions than they would otherwise receive if negotiating individually. The effect on the average worker—unionized or not—of working in a right-to-work state is to earn approximately $1,500 less per year than a similar worker in a state without such a law.

Workers in right-to-work states are also significantly less likely to receive employer-provided health insurance or pensions. If benefits coverage in non-right-to-work states were lowered to the levels of states with these laws, 2 million fewer workers would receive health insurance and 3.8 million fewer workers would receive pensions nationwide.

The fact that unionization raises people's wages and benefits is borne out by surveys of union members and by common sense. Unions also affect the wages and benefits of nonunion workers by setting standards that gradually become norms throughout industries. To compete for workers, nonunion employers in highly unionized industries have to pay their workers higher wages. And unions support government policies (such as minimum-wage laws) that raise workers' pay.

Right-to-work laws also may hurt workplace safety. For instance, the occupational-fatality rate in the construction industry—one of the most hazardous in terms of workplace deaths—is 34 percent higher in right-to-work states than in states without such laws. And one academic study finds that increasing union density has a positive effect on workplace safety in states with no right-to-work laws (for every 1 percent increase in unionization rates there is a 0.35 percent decline in construction fatality rates), but in right-to-work states, the effect of union density on safety disappears.

Unions are democratic organizations: If employees didn't like their contracts, they would vote to reject the contract, vote to change their union officers, or vote to get rid of their union—all of which can be done under current law.

Right-to-Work Laws Weaken the Middle Class

By weakening unions right-to-work laws also weaken the middle class. From pushing for fair wages and good benefits, to encouraging citizens to vote, to supporting Social Security and advocating for family-leave benefits, unions make the middle class strong by giving workers a voice in both the market and our democracy.

Nine of the 10 states with the lowest percentage of workers in unions—Mississippi, Arkansas, South Carolina, North Carolina, Georgia, Virginia, Tennessee, Texas, and Oklahoma—are right-to-work states. All of them also are saddled with a relatively weak middle class. The share of total income going to the middle class—defined as the middle 60 percent of the population—in each of these states is below the national average.

If unionization rates increased by 10 percentage points nationwide, the typical middle-class household—unionized or not—would earn $1,479 more each year. In fact, dollar for dollar, strengthening unions is nearly as important to the middle class as boosting college-graduation rates.

Right-to-Work Laws Hurt Small Business

Since few small businesses are ever unionized, changing union regulations won't affect them. Yet unlike big manufacturers who can choose which state to expand into, most small businesses are rooted in a local community and dependent on local consumers. When right-to-work laws lower the wages and benefits of area workers, they also threaten to reduce the number of jobs in the economy by reducing consumer demand.

THE CASE FOR MANDATORY UNION FEES GOES TO THE HIGH COURT

On Monday, we previewed a case the Supreme Court is set to hear on January 11th challenging the regime whereby public-sector employees have no choice but to pay union dues. The plaintiffs are teachers who refuse to join the California Teachers Association (CTA), the union that bargains on their behalf, and want to stop paying the "agency fees" that the CTA bills to non-members. They say that since negotiating with the government over salary, benefits and working conditions is "quintessentially political," it is a violation of dissenting teachers' freedom of speech to be coerced to pay "tribute" to unions undertaking that bargaining. In the previous post, we analysed the aggrieved teachers' brief to the justices. Now we will consider the respondents' arguments in favour of the arrangement that governs public-sector unions in nearly half of the states.

There are two parties to *Friedrichs v California Teachers Association* who rise in defence of "agency fees," also known as "fair-share fees": a collection of teachers unions and Kamala Harris, the attorney general of California. The two briefs track similar terrain, though the attorney general's brief takes more time to lay out the state's interest in "permitting employees to bargain collectively through one representative, funded by all represented employees."

"The Case for Mandatory Union Fees," The Economist Newspaper Limited, January 7, 2016.

The Economic Policy Institute estimates that for every $1 million in wage cuts, six jobs are lost in the service, retail, construction, real estate, and other local industries. For big manufacturers that sell their products all over the globe, this may be less important.

For small businesses that depend on local sales, reducing the amount of disposable income in local employees' pockets can be devastating.

Right-to-Work Laws Create Rules That Would Hurt All Organizations but Only Apply to Unions

The corporate lobbyists who push for right-to-work legislation—such as the Chamber of Commerce and the National Right to Work Committee—want unions to operate under a set of rules that none of them accept for themselves. These lobbyists would never think of serving the interests of companies that refuse to pay dues to their organizations, yet they want unions to do so in order to drain their resources.

Federal law already guarantees every worker who is represented by a union equal and nondiscriminatory representation—meaning unions must provide the same services, vigorous advocacy, and contractual rights and benefits. This guarantee applies regardless of whether the employee is a union member. So if a non-dues-paying employee encounters a problem at work, the union is required to provide that individual full representation at no charge.

By contrast, the Chamber of Commerce and other employer organizations restrict some of their most valuable services to dues-paying members. When asked if they would agree to provide all services to any interested business, even if that business does not pay dues, Chamber representatives explained that they could not do that because dues are the primary source of Chamber funding and it would be unfair to other dues-paying members. And that certainly makes sense—for unions as well as the Chamber.

The Chamber of Commerce and National Right to Work Committee want unions to be the only organizations in the country that are required to provide full services to individuals who pay nothing for them. This is no different than enabling some American citizens to opt out of paying taxes while making available all government services. This is not an agenda to increase employee rights but rather to undermine the viability of independent-employee organizations.

Right-to-Work Laws Are Bad for Our Political Democracy

Right-to-work laws infringe on the democratic rights of the electorate by weakening unions. Unions help boost political participation among ordinary citizens and convert this participation into an effective voice for pro-middle-class policies. By weakening unions, they are less able to advocate for pro-worker policies within our government and help get workers out to vote.

Research shows that for every percentage-point increase in union density, voter turnout increased by 0.2 to 0.25 percentage points. This means that if unionization rates were 10 percentage points higher during the 2008 presidential election, 2.6 million to 3.2 million more citizens would have voted.

Unions also help translate workers' interests to elected officials and ensure that government serves the economic needs of the middle class. They do this by encouraging the public to support certain policies as well as by directly advocating for specific reforms. Unions were critical in securing government policies that support the middle class such as Social Security, the Affordable Care Act, family leave, and minimum-wage laws.

Indeed, this may be a large part of why many conservatives support right-to-work laws. Research demonstrates that supporters' claims that these laws will create jobs and strengthen local economies are not credible. Instead, supporters may back these laws as a pretext for attacking an already weakened union movement in hopes of crippling it as a political force and as an advocate for all workers.

The bottom line: Right-to-work laws work against the critical needs of our economy, our society, and our democracy.

> *"Any worker accused by a union of being a free rider can argue, with just as much rigor, that he or she is a forced rider."*

Right-to-Work Laws Interfere with Freedom

Charles Baird

In the following viewpoint, Charles Baird begins with a quote from twentieth-century economist Milton Friedman, then goes on to argue that when unions aren't voluntary they violate a worker's right to free association as guaranteed by the US Constitution. This piece was written in 2006 and gives a good background on the libertarian arguments in support of right-to-work legislation. When Baird refers to "classical liberalism" he is referring to an economic philosophy that is a type of libertarianism. At the time of this writing, Charles Baird was a professor of economics emeritus at California State University at East Bay.

As you read, consider the following questions:

1. Baird's argument relies on a distinction between democracy in society and democracy in a workplace. How does he establish the difference?
2. How does Baird argue that right-to-work laws would not necessarily create the problem of "free riders" that many other viewpoints have discussed?
3. In what way does Baird say that "costs and benefits [of being represented by a union] are inherently subjective"?

T he principles involved in right-to-work laws are identical with those involved in [workplace anti-discrimination laws.] Both interfere with the freedom of the employment contract, in the one case by specifying that a particular color or religion cannot be made a condition of employment; in the other that membership in a union cannot be. —MILTON FRIEDMAN, 1962

Since Friedman penned those words in *Capitalism & Freedom* (p. 115), union apologists have claimed him as an ally in their campaign to ban right-to-work (RTW) laws in the United States. Section 14(b) of the National Labor Relations Act (NLRA) permits states to pass RTW laws, which prohibit employers and unions from agreeing to include union-security clauses in their collective-bargaining agreements. A union-security clause forces all workers represented by a union to pay fees (dues) for its services. Unions have attempted unsuccessfully to repeal Section 14(b) since its enactment in 1947. Now the National Right to Work Committee is attempting to get Congress to enact a National Right to Work Act. Are RTW laws consistent with the freedom philosophy?

If unions were voluntary associations that represented only their voluntary members, and if bargaining were wholly voluntary, there could be no classical-liberal objection to a union agreeing with a willing employer to adopt a union-security clause. The employer and the union would be free to choose whether to bargain over and to consent to such an arrangement, and workers would be free to choose, on an individual basis, whether to accept employment on such terms. Such is the common law of contracts. Under these circumstances a classical liberal should oppose RTW laws.

However, under Section 9(a) of the NLRA, American unions are not organizations that represent only their voluntary members. If they are certified by majority vote among workers in a bargaining unit they become the exclusive (monopoly) bargaining agents of all workers in the unit, whether individuals agree or not. Individuals are even forbidden to represent themselves. This is usually justified on grounds of "workplace democracy." As F. A. Hayek wrote in 1949 ("The Intellectuals and Socialism"), this is an example of "making shibboleths out of abstractions." The First Amendment forbids deciding which church to attend on the basis of a majority vote enforced by government. Likewise, the First Amendment's principle of freedom of association forbids deciding which representative will represent all workers on the basis of a majority vote enforced by government. Democracy is a form of government. Government cannot rightly impose democracy on private decision-making. In the private sphere of human action, an individual's associations should not be subject to majority vote. Exclusive representation should be repealed.

Correctly understood freedom of association in private affairs has two parts: First, any person has a fundamental right to associate with any other *willing* person or persons for any purpose that does not trespass against the fundamental rights of third parties. This is often called the positive right of freedom of association. Second, any person has a fundamental right to refrain from association with any other person or persons no matter how fervently these others may desire such association. This is often called the negative right of freedom of association. Logically, without a negative freedom of association, the positive freedom of association is meaningless. If A cannot refuse to associate with B, A does not have the (positive) freedom to choose with whom to associate. Freedom of association is irreconcilable with coerced association.

Economists define a free rider as one who receives net benefits from a collective action and can avoid paying for them due to the inherent nonexcludability of some goods. Unions and their apologists use the free-rider problem to justify union security. They argue that since a certified union is forced by law to represent all workers in a bargaining unit whether they approve of the union or not, all such workers must be forced to pay the union. Otherwise, they would get the benefits of union representation for free, and that would be unfair to those workers who willingly pay union dues.

However, there is nothing inherent in any employment relationship that gives rise to a free-rider problem. It is an artifact of the NLRA. Congress created the free-rider problem in labor relations through exclusive representation. If a union bargained only for its voluntary members, only they would benefit. Other workers would be free to designate some other willing third party to represent them or to choose to represent themselves. If unions want to eliminate the possibility of any worker being a free rider, they should advocate repeal of exclusive representation. Without exclusive representation there would be no need for a National Right to Work Act because the question of union security would be moot.

The unions' free-rider argument amounts to saying that since Congress has violated individual workers' freedom of association with exclusive representation, Congress must also override individual workers' freedom of association regarding support of unions that represent them. According to union apologists, one violation of freedom of association compels another violation of freedom of association. I argue that, given the first trespass against freedom of association, a National Right to Work Act is a proper way to avoid the second trespass.

Forced Support Justified?

Many argue that exclusive representation is a fact of life that we all must accept. Therefore, forcing workers to support unions is justified. However, even with exclusive representation, it can never be proven that any worker free-rides on any collective-bargaining agreement. A forced rider is one who suffers net harms from some collective action and who is compelled to pay for them. Even if one grants that unions can raise the wages and salaries that are paid to some workers, it does not follow that even those workers, on a net basis, gain from union actions. Costs and benefits are inherently subjective. Suppose a worker gets a $10 wage increase due to a union's representation. No third party can prove that this benefits the worker more than, less than, or the same as the cost imposed by, for example, the disutility the worker suffers from being forced to associate with the union. Any worker accused by a union of being a free rider can argue, with just as much rigor, that he or she is a forced rider. It is a conceit to argue that Congress or any other third party can make that determination for any worker.

In sum we live a second-best world. If there were no NLRA classical liberals should oppose right-to-work. The ideal policy prescription from a classical-liberal perspective is to repeal the NLRA. Until that happens, in my view a classical liberal is justified in supporting RTW laws.

> "In fact, the rights of all workers,
> regardless of their interest
> in unionization, are being
> whittled down."

The Law Does Not Support Workers' Rights

Martin Hart-Landsberg

In the following viewpoint, Martin Hart-Landsberg starts out by reminding readers that organizing a union is a protected right in the United States. However, he argues, companies rarely face consequences for violating this right. In addition, he says, the law is continually "whittling away" this right. He discusses several laws in addition to right-to-work laws that limit the rights of unions and union organizers and says that the only way to protect workers' rights in this environment is with strong rank and file organization and activism. Martin Hart-Landsberg is a professor of economics and director of the Political Economy Program at Lewis and Clark College in Portland, Oregon.

"The Law Versus Worker Rights," by Martin Hart-Landsberg, Monthly Review Foundation, November 10, 2018. Reprinted by permission.

As you read, consider the following questions:

1. How does the corporate practice of subcontracting make it more difficult for unions to protest unfair treatment?
2. How does this viewpoint explain that workers covered under the NLRA can lose rights that other workers have?
3. How did Jacob Lewis void his right to redress from his employer, according to the viewpoint?

Organizing a union is no easy task in the United States. Although organizing a union is supposed to be a protected right, businesses regularly fire union supporters knowing that they face minimal punishment even if found guilty for their actions. In fact, the rights of all workers, regardless of their interest in unionization, are being whittled down. Simply put, US law doesn't work for workers.

Moshe Z. Marvit, writing in the newspaper *In These Times*, provides a recent example of the ongoing legal attack on union rights, in this case those of unionized janitors. As he explains, the National Labor Relations Board, using a provision of the 1947 Taft-Hartley Act designed to weaken labor solidarity:

> ruled [in October 2018] that janitors in San Francisco violated the law when they picketed in front of their workplace to win higher wages, better working conditions and freedom from sexual harassment in their workplace.

The provision in question is one that prohibits workers from engaging in actions against a so-called "secondary" employer. The provision makes it illegal for workers to organize boycotts or pickets directed against an employer with which the union does not have a dispute in order to get that firm to pressure the union's employer to settle its dispute with the union.

The NLRB's ruling dramatically stretches the meaning of this provision, in that the San Francisco janitors were actually engaged in workplace actions against an employer that had significant influence over their terms of employment. However, Board members were able to justify their ruling thanks to the complexities generated by the increasingly common corporate strategy of subcontracting.

In this case, the janitors were employed by Ortiz Janitorial Services, which was in turn subcontracted by Preferred Building Services, to work in the building of yet a third company. An administrative law judge had previously ruled that Preferred Building Services had meaningful control over the employment terms of the janitors hired by Ortiz Janitorial Services.

More specifically, the judge found "that Preferred Building Services was involved in the hiring, firing, disciplining, supervision, direction of work, and other terms and conditions of the janitors' employment with Ortiz Janitorial Services." That made Ortiz and Preferred joint employers of the janitors, and the worker's actions legal. Undeterred, the NLRB simply rejected the administrative law judge's ruling, declaring instead that the janitors worked only for Ortiz which made the worker's actions, which were also aimed at Preferred, illegal.

As Marvit summarizes:

> The NLRB's recent case restricting the picketing rights of subcontractors, temps and other workers who do not have a single direct employment relationship is a further sign that the labor board will continue limiting its joint employer doctrine. This will make it more difficult or even impossible for many workers to have any meaningful voice in the workplace. But the case also highlights some of the core problems of labor law as it currently exists. By being included under the NLRA, workers lose basic rights that all other Americans enjoy.

Given how important the use of subcontracted labor has become, it should surprise no one that Trump's appointees to the National Labor Relations Board are actively working to tighten the standard under which workers can claim to face, and organize against, a joint employer.

But the attack on worker rights is not limited to efforts to weaken union power. The Supreme Court, in a 5-4 vote in May, ruled in *Epic Systems Corp v. Lewis*, that employers can include a clause in their employment contract requiring nonunion workers to arbitrate their disputes individually, a ruling that eliminates the ability of workers to sue a company for workplace violations or use collective actions such as class action suits. The ruling resolved three separate cases—*Epic Systems Corp. v. Lewis*, *Ernst & Young LLP v. Morris*, and *National Labor Relations Board v. Murphy Oil USA*—that were argued together in front of the Court on the same day because they all raised the same basic issue.

Marvit explains what led to Lewis's decision to sue Epic Systems:

> On April 2, 2014, Jacob Lewis, who was a technical writer for Epic Systems, received an email from his employer with a document titled "Mutual Arbitration Agreement Regarding Wages and Hours." The document stated that the employee and the employer waive their rights to go to court and instead agreed to take all wage and hour claims to arbitration. Furthermore, unlike in court, the employee agreed that any arbitration would be one-on-one. This "agreement" did not provide any opportunity to negotiate, and it had no place to sign or refuse to sign. Instead, it stated, "I understand that if I continue to work at Epic, I will be deemed to have accepted this Agreement." The workers had two choices: immediately quit or accept the agreement. . . .
>
> When Lewis tried to take Epic Systems to court for misclassifying him and his fellow workers as independent contractors and depriving them of overtime pay, he realized that by opening the email and continuing to work, he waved his right to bring a collective action or go to court.

As the Court saw it, the case pitted the Federal Arbitration Act against the National Labor Relations Act. The former established a legal foundation for using one-on-one arbitration to settle disputes while the latter gives workers the right to work together for "mutual aid and protection." The Court's ruling priviledged arbitration.

Jane McAlevey, writing before the Supreme Court combined the cases and decided *Epic Systems Corp v. Lewis*, highlights the likely anti-worker consequences of the Court's decision:

> As for loud liberal voices—union and nonunion—that declare unions as a thing of the past, the forthcoming SCOTUS ruling on *NLRB v Murphy Oil* will prove most of the nonunion "innovations" moot. Murphy Oil is a complicated legal case that boils down to removing what are called the Section 7 protections under the National Labor Relations Act, and preventing class action lawsuits.
>
> Murphy Oil blows a hole through the legal safeguards that nonunion workers have enjoyed for decades, eviscerating much of the tactical repertoire of so-called Alt Labor, such as class-action wage-theft cases, and workers participating in protests called by nonunion community groups in front of their workplaces. The timing is horrific and uncanny: As women are finally finding their voices about sexual harassment at work, mostly in nonunion workplaces (as the majority are), Murphy Oil will prevent class action sexual harassment lawsuits.

The Epic Systems decision is a big deal, since there is a growing and already sizeable use of mandatory arbitration by employers. A study by the Economic Policy Institute found that:

- More than half—53.9 percent—of nonunion private-sector employers have mandatory arbitration procedures. Among companies with 1,000 or more employees, 65.1 percent have mandatory arbitration procedures.
- Among private-sector nonunion employees, 56.2 percent are subject to mandatory employment arbitration procedures. Extrapolating to the overall workforce, this means that 60.1 million American workers no longer have access to the courts to protect their legal employment rights and instead must go to arbitration.
- Of the employers who require mandatory arbitration, 30.1 percent also include class action waivers in their

procedures—meaning that in addition to losing their right to file a lawsuit on their own behalf, employees also lose the right to address widespread rights violations through collective legal action.

- Large employers are more likely than small employers to include class action waivers, so the share of employees affected is significantly higher than the share of employers engaging in this practice: of employees subject to mandatory arbitration, 41.1 percent have also waived their right to be part of a class action claim. Overall, this means that 23.1 percent of private-sector nonunion employees, or 24.7 million American workers, no longer have the right to bring a class action claim if their employment rights have been violated.
- Mandatory arbitration is more common in low-wage workplaces. It is also more common in industries that are disproportionately composed of women workers and in industries that are disproportionately composed of African American workers.

The Court's decision means that workers without unions will have little power. The NLRB's decision weakens the laws that are supposed to protect union rights. The only effective response to this trend is, as the recent wave of teacher strikes demonstrated, militant, rank and file-led union organizing, with strong community involvement and support. Hopefully, exposing the class-biased nature of US laws may help encourage this kind of activism.

> "One way to understand the real intent of RTW is to imagine what would happen to the public services in one's town, city or state if the payment of taxes were voluntary. How long would our public schools, libraries, sanitation systems, water facilities, parks and so forth function if taxes were optional?"

Right-to-Work Laws Create Union Free Riders

Roland Zullo

In the following viewpoint, written just after Wisconsin passed right-to-work legislation, Roland Zullo explains in some detail what these laws are and are not, this time with some historical background and an explanation of the aspect of US labor law that makes this kind of legislation possible. The author goes on to explain why he and others believe that "right to freeload" would be a more appropriate name for these laws. Roland Zullo is a research scientist at the Institute for Research on Labor, Employment and the Economy at the University of Michigan.

As you read, consider the following questions:

1. How are right-to-work laws like giving citizens the chance to opt-out of paying taxes according to the viewpoint?
2. What was the intent of the original labor laws?
3. For what do labor organizations use member fees?

An effort to weaken organized labor is sweeping the Midwest, a region with a rich history of union activism.

The strategy takes advantage of a curious provision of US labor law, section 14 (b). It allows states to pass laws that prohibit unions from negotiating the collection of union dues with employers and, more specifically, from compelling workers covered by the bargaining agreement to pay them as a condition of employment.

Under labor law, employees that do not pay dues enjoy the same wages, benefits and protections as those who do. A labor union that discriminates against someone covered by the contract (and who doesn't pay dues) is liable to a duty of fair representation lawsuit.

Corporations call these laws "right-to-work" (RTW). Unions prefer the term "right-to-freeload" (RTF).

Wisconsin last month became the latest (and 25th) state to pass legislation that allows union-covered workers to refrain from paying dues. Legislators in Illinois, Missouri, Kentucky and New Mexico are agitating to following suit.

What do these laws mean for organized labor?

What RTW Isn't About

First, let us begin by anticipating and then dismissing several pretexts. RTW is not about granting workers the freedom to associate, as supporters argue. If that were the case, then RTW advocates would approach the minority union concept, keenly argued by Charles Morris in *The Blue Eagle at Work: Reclaiming Democratic Rights in the American Workplace*, with equal zeal.

Morris explains that the intent of the original labor law was to promote collective bargaining by compelling employers to negotiate with groups of workers on behalf of members only, even if they did not constitute at least 50% of employees. Silence on this issue from right-to-work supporters undermines the credibility of the "freedom to associate" motive.

RTW is also not about making labor unions more responsive to workers by allowing them to withhold dues payments. The very same objective could be achieved by allowing union objectors to remit the equivalent of union dues to an agreed-upon charity, enabling workers to register dissatisfaction with a union without giving them a financial incentive to do so. Hence, the objection would genuinely reflect ideology or religious concerns, and not free-rider opportunism.

However, the American Legislative Council (ALEC)-sponsored legislation sweeping the nation expressly prohibits any requirement to "pay to any charity or other third party, in lieu of such payments, any amount equivalent to or a pro-rata portion of dues, fees, assessments, or other charges regularly required of members of a labor organization."

ALEC is a group of conservative state legislators that crafts "model" legislation and lobbies like-minded politicians to pass the bills, as has been the case with right-to-work.

What RTW Does

One way to understand the real intent of RTW is to imagine what would happen to the public services in one's town, city or state if the payment of taxes were voluntary. How long would our public schools, libraries, sanitation systems, water facilities, parks and so forth function if taxes were optional?

Charging fees would be impermissible, because persons that refuse to pay tax would have an equal right to the schools, libraries, garbage collection, water, etc, as those that do pay. Just like RTW, the services would have to remain equally accessible to tax payers as well as tax deadbeats. Public services as we know them would collapse.

All collective endeavors require resources to achieve their goals. Labor unions represent working persons at their place of employment through collective bargaining. Organized labor also has an admirable history of fighting on behalf of non-union workers through political advocacy on issues such as workplace safety, minimum wage and public health insurance. The obvious intent of the ALEC-funded RTW effort is to burden the union movement's pursuit of these goals by making it difficult to acquire financial resources.

Labor Free Riders

Evidence of a RTW burden is beginning to appear in state-level statistics.

The graph below provides trend lines for the union free rider percentages in Illinois, Indiana, Michigan and Wisconsin. The free rider percentage is the percent of persons in the state that are covered by a collective bargaining agreement but are not union members. The estimates are from the Current Population Survey administered by the Bureau of Labor Statistics.

Figure 1: Union Free Rider Percentages for Midwest US States

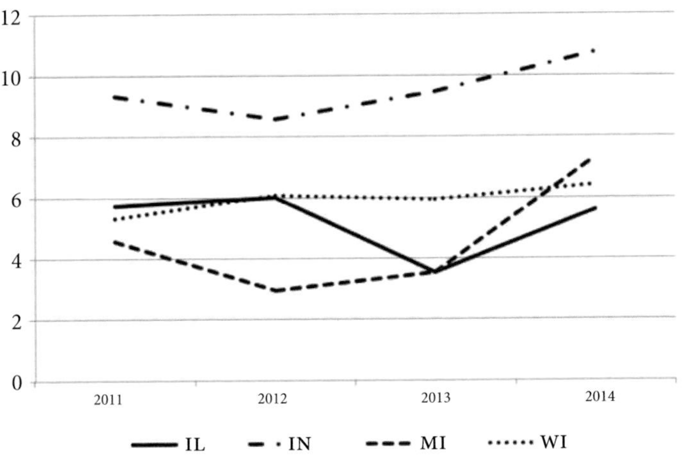

Source: Bureau of Labor Statistics

The top line is Indiana, which passed RTW in 2012. The dashed line at the bottom is Michigan, which passed RTW in late 2012, effective 2013. Both states show a gain in the percentages of free riders following the passage of RTW laws.

The growth in free riders for Michigan would have been even more dramatic had RTW applied immediately to all collective bargaining agreements. Prior to the law, many unions across the state signed binding letters of intent with their employers to extend union security provisions. As these letters expire, the RTW burden will predictably increase.

Wisconsin (dotted line) displays an upward trend in free ridership, although quite gradual by comparison with Indiana and Michigan. The trend in Wisconsin might be attributable to the evisceration of collective bargaining rights for public employees in 2011. The Midwest state that has experienced little change in bargaining law, Illinois (solid line), has a free rider rate from 4% to 6%, and no discernible trend over the period.

Elite Arrogance Back in Vogue?

It is important to not only acknowledge these trends but to understand the context that gives rise to RTW, or any other anti-worker policy. What does RTW symbolize?

On a political level, the expansion of RTW is symptomatic of the resurgent influence of corporate control over political affairs. Advocates for RTW, as agents of the corporate class, evidently have enough resources to convince persons to vote to undermine one of the few social institutions that advance the interests of working persons.

Observing these events brings to mind the quip attributed to the 19th-century railroad baron, Jay Gould, during an earlier era of great inequality: "I can hire one half of the working class to kill the other half." Elite arrogance is back in vogue.

Periodical and Internet Sources Bibliography

The following articles have been selected to supplement the diverse views presented in this chapter.

Mike Collins, "The Decline in Unions Is a Middle-Class Problem," *Forbes*, March 19, 2015. https://www.forbes.com/sites/mikecollins/2015/03/19/the-decline-of-unions-is-a-middle-class-problem/#2a8327e57f2d.

Haley Sweetland Edwards, "Supreme Court Deals Public Unions a Blow," *Time*, June 30, 2014. http://time.com/2940466/harris-quinn-supreme-court-labor-unions.

James Feigenbaum, Alexander Hertel-Fernandez, and Vanessa Williamson, "Right-to-Work Laws Have Devastated Unions—and Democrats," *New York Times*, March 8, 2018. https://www.nytimes.com/2018/03/08/opinion/conor-lamb-unions-pennsylvania.html.

Dwyer Gunn, "What Caused the Decline of Unions in America? Globalization, Politics, and the American Psyche Are All to Blame," *Pacific Standard*, April 24, 2018. https://psmag.com/economics/what-caused-the-decline-of-unions-in-america.

Jana Kasperkevic, "Why Unions Are So Worried About Right-to-Work Laws," *Marketplace*, February 24, 2017. https://www.marketplace.org/2017/02/24/business/push-nationwide-right-work-law-could-weaken-unions.

Raymond J. LaJeunesse Jr., "The Future Looks Bright for the Right-to-Work Movement," *Regulatory Review*, April 5, 2019. https://www.theregreview.org/2019/04/05/lajeunesse-right-to-work-movement.

Dana Millbank, "So Much for the Labor Movement's Funeral," *Washington Post*, January 25, 2019. https://www.washingtonpost.com/opinions/so-much-for-the-labor-movements-funeral/2019/01/25/53e5389c-20c3-11e9-9145-3f74070bbdb9_story.html?utm_term=.508cafa67825.

Andy Newbold, Alessandra Dimonda, and Brian Rabitz, "Myths and Facts About 'Right-To-Work' Laws," *Media Matters*, December 12, 2012. https://www.mediamatters.org/research/2012/12/12/myths-and-facts-about-right-to-work-laws/191810.

Robert Reich, "Strengthen Unions," RobertReich.org, May 28, 2015. https://robertreich.org/post/120107784670.

Neil Shah and Ben Casselman, "'Right-to-Work' Economics: States That Bar Mandatory Union Dues Tend Toward More Jobs but Lower Wages," *Wall Street Journal*, December 14, 2012. https://www.wsj.com/articles/SB10001424127887324296604578179603136860138.

OPPOSING
VIEWPOINTS®
SERIES

CHAPTER 5

Should the Minimum Wage Be Increased?

Chapter Preface

A minimum wage law sets the lowest hourly amount that workers can legally be paid. In 1938, with the passage of the Fair Labor Standards Act, the US Congress set the first federal minimum wage at twenty-five cents per hour. The federal minimum wage applies to all states. However, individual states, and even cities, can set higher standards, and in fact many US states and several cities have higher minimum wages than the federal.

Since 1938, Congress has raised the federal minimum wage more than twenty times. As of this writing it was $7.25 per hour. Automatic increases based on the cost of living are not a part of the law. Congress must pass a new law each time it wants to increase the minimum wage.

When adjusted for the cost of living, you find that in 1968, the minimum wage was worth $10.75 in 2019 dollars. In 1968, families could live comfortably on minimum wage, even if it took some creative grocery shopping. By 2019, that was virtually impossible. The minimum wage had fallen far behind the cost of living. For that reason, a strong movement to increase the minimum wage gained strength in the first couple of decades of the twenty-first century, and many states and cities did indeed raise it. However, in much of the country, the idea met a surprising amount of resistance.

The viewpoints in this chapter take on the issue of once again raising the minimum wage, in states and nationally. Arguments range from the purely economic to the social and moral. Some of the viewpoints here focus on the fact that many minimum-wage workers are young people who may not need to make as much money as older people raising families. Others point out that higher mandated wages makes it harder for low-skilled workers to get jobs of any kind. Some authors zero in on the economics of the issues, arguing that cheap labor is necessary for businesses to stay afloat. Some say that guaranteeing workers the right to a living wage is a moral imperative—that no matter what its effects on the economy, it is the right thing to do.

> "*Even if the wages of these Walmart employees reached the 'lofty' $15 an hour sought by labor groups, they would still be a far cry from what is necessary to raise a family in this country and significantly less than the median household income.*"

Walmart's Pay Raise Was Good, but Middle-Income Workers Need More Help

Mechele Dickerson

In the following viewpoint, Mechele Dickerson examines the announcement, in 2015, that Walmart was increasing the wages of its lowest-paid workers. It also agreed to make work schedules more predictable. Dickerson points out that as the largest private employer in the United States, the retailer has an outsized influence on both the government and other retailers, and that the decision had the potential to result in similar raises for other middle-income workers. However, the author argues that this will not be enough to solve the problems of America's middle class. Mechele Dickerson is a professor of law at the University of Texas, Austin. She specializes in exploring the causes, consequences, and shifting perceptions of consumer debt.

As you read, consider the following questions:

1. Why did Walmart say that it increased wages?
2. Dickerson says Walmart's decision was significant because Walmart itself made the announcement. Why did that matter?
3. What is the real reason middle-income workers are struggling, according to the viewpoint?

W almart recently did something that will help its employees, which may very well benefit all lower- and middle-income workers in this country. The "something" is not the wage increase its lowest-paid workers will soon receive. Instead, the thing that Walmart did that should help lower-paid workers was to announce that it was doing anything at all.

Walmart has agreed to pay about 500,000 of its least-paid employees at least $9 an hour starting in April and at least $10 starting next February—a significant raise from the $7.25 federal minimum wage they currently earn. The retailer also said that it will change its policies to make it easier for employees to have a stable and more predictable work schedule.

While the moves may be laudable and should be replicated at other retailers, they mainly serve to remind us how desperate is the plight of America's working class. Even if the wages of these Walmart employees reached the "lofty" $15 an hour sought by labor groups, they would still be a far cry from what is necessary to raise a family in this country and significantly less than the median household income.

Still, it's a start.

A Skeptical Response

Walmart's announcement was met with plenty of skepticism, with many assuming that the pay hike had more to do with politics or avoiding more labor action than concern for its employees. For example, critics argued that Walmart was attempting to stymie

Total Worker Compensation Not Increasing as Economy Recovers

The Federal Reserve Board, along with most economists, has been closely tracking the rate of increase in the average hourly wage reported by the Bureau of Labor Statistics in its monthly employment report. This series has shown a modest uptick in growth over the last two years. While the current pace (2.5 percent over the last year) is only slightly above the Fed's 2.0 percent inflation target, it actually overstates the extent to which workers are benefiting from the recovery.

While wage growth has accelerated modestly from its pace earlier in the recovery, the rate of growth in benefits, most importantly healthcare, has slowed. As a result, there has been almost no change in the rate of growth in total compensation.

This can be seen by comparing the rate of growth of the average hourly wage series with the growth in the Employment Cost Index (ECI). The ECI series also has separate wage and benefit components. [The average hourly wage series is for production and non-supervisory workers since the overall series does not go back before 2000.]

The modest acceleration in wage growth has been accompanied by a slowing in the growth of benefits, leading to almost no change in the rate of growth of total compensation. In short, we are not seeing any evidence of an acceleration in compensation growth; instead, we are seeing a shift in the composition of compensation from benefits to wages.

legislative proposals to raise the minimum wage. Or that it was trying to stifle employee and labor organizers' demands that the company pay all workers at least $15 an hour.

Walmart has candidly admitted that it acted in part because of a profit motive. The company concluded that it needed to increase wages and provide more secure work schedules in order to attract employees and reduce its high turnover rate.

Whatever Walmart's motives, the announcement is nonetheless seismic. Not because of the size of the pay raise or the reasons the company concluded it was time to give workers more predictable work schedules. Walmart's recent announcement is significant because Walmart made the announcement.

When Walmart Speaks, Everyone Listens

When the largest private employer in the country talks about anything—including the economic conditions of its lowest-paid workers—everybody listens. And, when Walmart speaks, the government, the media and other retail employers react, even though they might have largely ignored a similar announcement made by another business.

For example, while Walmart has long been criticized for refusing to give its employees predictable work schedules, other retailers follow similar policies.

Until last year, Starbucks' barristas also had unpredictable schedules and often were required to "clopen" stores, that is, close the store one night then return the next morning to open it. Like Walmart, Starbucks announced that it would voluntarily end this unpopular practice.

The Starbucks announcement was not as widely discussed or dissected as Walmart's, and few companies reacted to it by declaring they were considering a change to their own clopening policies.

In contrast, in the days following the Walmart news, everyone in the media was talking about it, and business analysts assumed that other retailers would be forced to re-evaluate what they pay their workers and how they set their work schedules. The predictions so far have proved right; retailer TJMaxx just announced that it will match the Walmart raises.

Perhaps one reason Starbucks did not generate the stir that Walmart did is because the coffee chain is a media darling, while everyone loves to hate the world's biggest retailer. It is more likely, though, that fewer businesses reacted to the Starbucks announcement because Starbucks just isn't Walmart.

Credit Where Credit Is Due

One thing that has been discounted in the rush to scrutinize, criticize and demonize Walmart's announcement is the unmistakable effect that the pay raise will have on a half-million American workers. The raise will help its lower-income workers spend more—and perhaps even save more.

These workers will soon earn well above the $7.25 federal minimum wage, though even the proposed 2016 hourly wage is less than the $10.10 federal minimum wage President Obama has recommended. Walmart has been criticized, perhaps fairly, for not raising its minimum hourly wage to the $15 "living wage" employee groups and labor organizers have urged.

Obviously, Walmart could have decided to pay its employees more and give its shareholders less and critics correctly note that Walmart's mass raise isn't enough to solve its workers' financial problems. But, that's mostly because the raise can't fix the real reason so many lower- and middle-income workers are struggling: the ever increasing gap between what lower- and middle-income Americans earn relative to what the highest paid Americans make.

Working Class Need So Much

Walmart's lowest-paid workers will soon earn about $22,000 a year. That annual income is enough to qualify as middle-income for a one-person household, but is about $30,000 less than overall US median household income. Even if these employees earned a minimum of $15 an hour, they would take home just $31,000 a year—still roughly $20,000 less than the median.

Criticism of Walmart may be fair, but the bigger problem is that the employees and most lower- and middle-wage workers need so much. Walmart's wage increase will help its lower-wage workers look a little more like middle-wage workers. But that's only because so many middle-wage jobs have disappeared over the last 30 years and many of the middle income jobs lost during the recession were replaced by low-wage jobs.

Since the recession, the strongest employment growth has continued to be in the retail, service and food/beverage sector. And fortunately, wage increases in 2014 were largest for lower-skilled, part-time workers.

Unfortunately, the lowest-paid Walmart workers—like low-skilled, low-wage workers overall—were hit so hard by the recession that these recent increases are doing little to help their economic mobility.

Because lower- and middle-income workers had increasingly small shares of income growth, they are actually beginning to look a lot like each other. Neither group, though, looks much like the highest-paid workers, who earned a disproportionate share of overall income growth since 1980. And no one looks like the top 1%, who saw their income increase by approximately 35% after the recession while wages for everybody else mostly stagnated.

Walmart's pay hike may just be a masterful public relations stunt. Even so, the announcement forced everybody to think about what lower-income workers need to survive and whether they can survive on the federal minimum wage, Walmart's minimum wage, or even President Obama's proposed minimum wage. And it forced at least one major retailer to follow suit and increase its employees' minimum wage.

Walmart alone can't solve the biggest problem lower- and middle-income workers in this country are facing. The retailer's lowest-paid workers will continue to struggle alongside their peers elsewhere until the country commits to finding ways to help them move up the economic ladder.

> *"The argument that only a small share of workers is actually paid the minimum wage misses a key point: many of those who would be impacted by a raise in the minimum wage are actually low-wage workers making slightly above the minimum wage."*

Minimum Wage Increases Have a Ripple Effect

Benjamin H. Harris and Melissa S. Kearney

In the following viewpoint, Benjamin H. Harris and Melissa S. Kearney address the argument that most minimum wage workers are teens and young adults who do not need to make a living wage. The authors find that most minimum wage workers are in fact older workers, and a minimum wage increase has a ripple-effect on workers earning slightly higher wages. Benjamin H. Harris is a visiting associate professor at the Kellogg School of Management at Northwestern University. He recently served as the chief economist and economic adviser to Vice President Joe Biden. Melissa S. Kearney is an economics professor at the University of Maryland and nonresident senior fellow at the Brookings Institute.

As you read, consider the following questions:

1. What is the "ripple effect" of minimum wage increases described in this viewpoint?
2. What is the "jobs gap" discussed here and how might closing it change the arguments for or against a minimum wage increase?
3. What impact of a minimum wage increase do the authors urge policy makers to take into consideration?

U S policymakers continue to engage in an active debate over the minimum wage. Calls for minimum wage increases—at the federal, state, and local levels—are based on the premise that rises in the minimum wage will improve the economic well-being of low-paid workers. This has become an important policy prescription in movements to combat poverty.

One area of focus in the debate is whether a minimum wage increase would actually affect many workers. Some skeptics have argued that only a very small share of workers actually receive the minimum wage, and furthermore, that many of those workers are not struggling adults, but rather teenagers from affluent families. Understanding the magnitude of the impact of a federal or state-level minimum wage increase on workers is an important first step in informing the policy debate.

The argument that only a small share of workers is actually paid the minimum wage misses a key point: many of those who would be impacted by a raise in the minimum wage are actually low-wage workers making slightly above the minimum wage. In addition to this broader scope of the workforce, economist Arin Dube of the University of Massachusetts-Amherst points out that a shrinking share of low-wage workers is comprised of teenagers. His work shows that among those earning no more than the federal minimum wage of $7.25 in 2011, fewer than a quarter were teenagers. Among those earning less than $10 an hour, only 12 percent were teenagers, as compared to 26 percent in 1979.

4 Reasons the Minimum Wage Should Not Be Raised

From a worker's viewpoint, raising minimum wage would seem to carry a number of benefits. Opponents disagree, claiming that an increase only means employers must pay more money to less skilled workers while at the same time expecting more from the employees. For a variety of reasons, higher minimum wages may actually work against the best interests of businesses, workers and customers as well.

Makes College Less Appealing

According to Max Borders in an article written for the *Washington Examiner* in March 2011, roughly half of all minimum wage workers are 24 and under, and teenagers alone comprise nearly 25 percent. Better minimum wages for workers in this age range may prove a deterrent to getting a college education. When faced with the choice of earning an immediate income or the potential of a better income after four or more years of additional schooling, young people tend to lean towards the former, says corporate-law scholar Stephen Bainbridge.

Low Impact

Opponents of increasing minimum wage believe that doing so accomplishes little in the way of reducing poverty. The population of minimum wage workers is relatively small when compared to other

In this month's Hamilton Project economic analysis, we consider the likely magnitude of the effects of a minimum wage increase on the number and share of workers affected. Considering that near-minimum wage workers would also be affected, we find that an increase could raise the wages of up to 35 million workers— that's 29.4 percent of the workforce. For the purpose of this analysis, we set aside the important issue of potential employment effects, which is another crucial element in the debate about an optimal minimum wage policy. We also continue to explore the nation's members of the working force, so only a select group of individuals benefit from the change. Additionally, a raised minimum wage does nothing for those who are unemployed to begin with.

Hurts Unemployment Rates

Some companies, especially in the case of small business, are less likely to hire employees if minimum wage is raised. Since the cost of hiring an untrained worker is higher, companies may elect to work with smaller staffs instead of taking the financial hit of running at full capacity. This in turn leads to unskilled workers having a harder time finding jobs, sending unemployment rates up and hurting the economy in the process.

Raises Prices

If businesses are forced to pay more to employ workers, budgets are affected accordingly. To help with the bottom line, prices may go up as a way of retaining money spent on providing extra compensation to minimum wage workers. Companies are essentially forced between losing money or risking dissatisfied customers by increasing prices, which ultimately means lower profits either way. If a business does manage to keep up financially, it's the customers that suffer. If the business fails, the workers suffer.

"Reasons Why the Minimum Wage Should Not Be Raised," by Spencer Hendricks, Leaf Group Ltd, 2019.

"jobs gap," or the number of jobs needed to return to pre-recession employment levels.

The Ripple Effects of Minimum Wage Policy

Although relatively few workers report wages exactly equal to (or below) the minimum wage, a much larger share of workers in the United States earns wages near the minimum wage. This holds true in the states that comply with the federal minimum wage, in addition to those states that have instituted their own higher minimum wage levels.

An increase in the minimum wage tends to have a "ripple effect" on other workers earning wages near that threshold. This ripple effect occurs when a raise in the minimum wage increases the wage received by workers earning slightly above the minimum wage. This effect of the statutory minimum wage on wages paid at the low end of the wage distribution more generally is well recognized in the academic literature. Based on this recognition, we quantify the number of workers potentially affected by minimum wage policy using the assumption that workers earning up to 150 percent of the minimum wage would see a wage increase from a higher minimum wage. We hasten to note that a complete analysis of the net effects of a minimum wage increase would also have to account for potential negative employment effects. Our main goal of this empirical exercise is to dispel the notion that the minimum wage is not a relevant policy lever, which is based on the faulty premise that only a small number of workers would be affected.

Using data from the Bureau of Labor Statistics, combined with information on the binding minimum wage in each state, we are able to calculate these shares. Just 2.6 percent of workers are paid exactly the minimum wage, but 29.4 percent of workers are paid wages that are below or equal to 150 percent of the minimum wage in their state. Furthermore, the hours worked by this group represent nearly one-quarter—24.7 percent—of hours worked, which indicates that a large share of the impacted group is working close to full time hours.

In 2012, 32 states complied with the federally set minimum wage of $7.25 per hour. In these states adhering to the federal floor, 3.7 million workers earn the minimum wage or less. An additional 15.2 million are near minimum wage, earning more than $7.25 per hour but less than $10.88 per hour. Therefore, 18.9 million workers in these states would likely benefit from an increase in the federal minimum wage.

The Ripple Effect by State

States have the opportunity to set a minimum wage above the federal floor. Eighteen states, plus the District of Columbia, had minimum wages that exceeded the federal wage floor in 2012, ranging from $7.40 in Michigan and Rhode Island to $9.04 in Washington. In these states, 3.9 million workers earn their state's minimum wage and an additional 12.1 million workers earn between the mandated floor but less than 150 percent of the minimum level.

Overall, up to 16.0 million workers would likely see a raise in their wages if the minimum wage were increased in these states.

Indeed, every state in the country has a substantial share of workers who would be impacted by an increase in the minimum wage in that state. In 2012, Montana had the highest share of workers—37.2 percent—with wages equal to or less than 150 percent of the minimum wage. Even in Alaska, which boasts higher wages compared to the rest of the country, 16.9 percent of workers had wages equal to or lower than 150 percent of the minimum. In the high-population state of California, 4.6 million workers would likely see a wage increase if the minimum wage were raised in that state.

Not surprisingly, the eighteen states with a higher minimum wage level than the federal benchmark tended to have higher shares of workers with wages within 150 percent of the minimum wage. However, in every state in the country, at least one in six workers had wages that were equal to 150 percent of the minimum wage or lower.

The December Jobs Gap

As of December, our nation faces a jobs gap of 7.8 million jobs. If the economy adds about 208,000 jobs per month, which was the average monthly rate for the best year of job creation in the

2000s, then it will take until September 2018 to close the jobs gap. Given a more optimistic rate of 321,000 jobs per month, which was the average monthly rate of the best year of job creation in the 1990s, the economy will reach pre-recession employment levels by August 2016.

Conclusion

The minimum wage debate currently underway tends to narrowly focus on those workers making exactly the minimum wage. This approach misses a large number of low-wage workers whose wages would likely be raised through a ripple effect resulting from an increase in the minimum wage.

As our economy continues to recover, a minimum wage increase could provide a much-needed boost to the earnings of low-wage workers. A significant 35 million workers from across the country could see their wages rise if the minimum wage were increased, allowing them to earn a better livelihood and lead more economically secure lives. When discussing the minimum wage, this is the magnitude of the impact that policymakers should consider.

NOTE: Throughout this analysis we only consider non-self-employed workers age 16-64. By our calculations, the size of that workforce was 122.2 million workers in 2012.

> *"Higher labor costs render low-skilled workers unemployable as it removes their key competitive advantage—cost. As a result, they are being replaced by machines."*

Minimum Wage Hikes Cause Businesses to Cut Jobs

Stephen McBride

In the following viewpoint, Stephen McBride cites examples of US fast-food companies that cut hours and increased use of automation in response to minimum wage increases mandated by their states. Other, smaller restaurants, he said, simply went out of business. He then cites data showing that many companies are increasing automation in their workplaces and concludes that minimum wage increases will do more harm than good for individual workers, mostly younger, unskilled ones. Stephen McBride is a writer and editor who writes about economic issues.

As you read, consider the following questions:

1. The author cites examples of negative effects on the economy due to minimum wage increases. What did then governor of California Jerry Brown say about that?
2. What particular age worker does the author focus on?
3. Why does this author think it is unlikely that companies will cut margins in response to rising labor costs?

In January, 19 US states raised their respective minimum wages. Washington was among the most generous, hiking by $1.53 (bringing it to $11 per hour). Arizona got an increase of $1.95—their "bottom rung" now sits at $10 per hour.

In all, 4.3 million workers are slated to receive a hike as they earn less than the new minimum wage in their respective states. Well, that's what's meant to happen. Judging by the fallout from recent hikes, it seems things aren't going according to plan.

Minimum Wage Massacre

In February, Wendy's CEO Bob Wright said the firm expects wages to rise at least 4% in 2017. Wendy's has three options to offset the rising costs.

First, they could cut margins, but with an 8% margin, that's unlikely. The second option is to raise prices. Given how price-sensitive consumers are these days, that too is a non-starter. Finally, the firm could reduce the amount of labor they use… and that's exactly what they did. Wendy's eliminated 31 hours of labor per location, per week.

However, their locations are just as busy. To keep output steady, they are planning to install automated kiosks in 16% of their locations by the end of 2017. David Trimm, Wendy's CIO said the timeframe for payback on the machines would be less than two years, thanks to labor savings.

Market leader McDonald's has also been automating. Last November, the firm said every one of its 14,000 US stores will be replacing cashiers with automated kiosks. McDonald's has actually prioritized these changes in locations like Seattle and New York that have higher minimum wages.

The restaurant industry is the canary in the coal mine when it comes to raising the minimum wage. In 2015, two-thirds of workers earning minimum wage were employed in service occupations (mostly food preparation). Today, restaurants spend (on average) one-third of their revenue on labor.

Currently, rising labor costs are causing margins in the sector to plummet. Those with the ability to automate like McDonalds are doing so … and those who don't are closing their doors. In September 2016, one-quarter of restaurant closures in the California Bay Area cited rising labor costs as one of the reasons for closing.

With the restaurant industry flashing warning signs, what do higher minimum wages mean for the rest of the economy?

Labor Lockout

In 2015, the percentage of hourly paid workers earning the prevailing minimum wage was 3.3%. While this may not seem like a lot, young people are disproportionately impacted. Around 68% of these workers are between ages 16 and 34.

A key point is that in 2016, 20.6 million workers (30% of all hourly, non-self-employed workers 18 and older) were "near-minimum-wage workers." This means they earned more than the prevailing minimum wage but less than $10.10 per hour. Some states have already surpassed this level, with many more on an incremental path toward it.

While wage increases put more money in the pocket of some, others are bearing the costs by having their hours reduced and being made part-time.

A recent example of this is in Seattle. In 2015, the Rainy City raised its minimum wage from $9.47 to $11 per hour. The effects? A study from the University of Washington in 2016 found that it decreased low-wage employment by 1%.

The study also found that while median wages rose, this was largely due to a strong economy. It's important to note these increases don't happen in isolation. The cost of wage hikes can be masked by a strong economy.

The study went on to say that working hours were reduced as a result of the hike. Interesting, many individuals actually moved their residence to take jobs outside of the city "at an elevated rate compared to historical patterns."

The 2015 bill included a provision in which firms with over 500 employees must pay a $15 per hour minimum wage starting January 2017. For companies with under 500 employees, it's $13 per hour. Given this, Seattle is the closest thing there is to a controlled experiment on this topic.

With calls for further minimum wage increases likely to continue, what can we expect going forward?

Automation Annihilation

When signing a bill that will raise California's minimum wage to $15 per hour by 2022, Governor Jerry Brown was very observant. Brown said, "Economically, minimum wages may not make sense. But morally, socially and politically they make every sense."

Brown is correct about the political part, but otherwise swings a miss. This hike will increase the cost of labor. Therefore, some jobs will be priced out of existence and some workers will be out of jobs.

Unfortunately, those who will suffer most are the young and low-skilled… the very people such laws are meant to help. In fact, Governor Brown knows this well. In 2014, he said that raising the wage would "put a lot of poor people out of work."

There are also many studies that prove a rising minimum wage reduces low-skilled employment. This isn't a US phenomenon either. Across Europe, there are higher unemployment rates in countries that have minimum wages.

Higher labor costs render low-skilled workers unemployable as it removes their key competitive advantage—cost. As a result, they are being replaced by machines. This is part of the wider issue of automation.

A 2013 study from the University of Oxford concluded that 47% of jobs in the US will likely be automated over the next two decades.

A 2017 report by McKinsey that looked at the ability of machines to replace human labor drew the same conclusion. The report found that 59% of all manufacturing tasks could be automated using current technology. The most exposed sector is food service, where 73% of tasks could be automated.

The inflation-adjusted minimum wage peaked back in 1968. However, it seems to be doing more harm than ever today. This is partly because of technological advancement, which has accounted for 88% of the 5 million manufacturing jobs lost since 2000.

Unless we stop seeing "political-sense" attempts to raise minimum wages, we are likely to see a lot more Flippy's [fast food restaurants] very soon.

> *"The federal minimum wage keeps an entire class of people trapped in economic servitude, focusing their attention on survival rather than growth, barring their ability to save enough or pay for education that would allow them to rise to the middle class."*

Low Wages Cost the Government Money

Heidi Moore

Previous viewpoints have focused on the larger economic view of the minimum wage. In the following viewpoint, Heidi Moore concentrates on the effects low wages have on individual workers. When people earn less than it takes to buy food and pay for health care, they are often forced to accept government benefits. This costs the government money. Businesses, on the other hand, profit from the arrangement, the author says. Heidi Moore is a digital media adviser. She has been economics editor at the Guardian *and a financial reporter at the* Wall Street Journal.

As you read, consider the following questions:

1. What limits does a low minimum wage put on workers, according to the viewpoint?
2. Why is an excessively low minimum wage costly to the government?
3. Why is offering benefits as important to the economy as increasing wages, according to the author?

You'd think the exceptionally low minimum wage—$7.25 an hour—would be the shame of a country like the United States that prides itself on its economic leadership. Half of minimum-wage jobs are held by adults over 25 years old, and asking adults to live on $7.25, or $14,500 a year, doesn't leave them with enough to rent an apartment, commute to work, raise a child and participate in society in any meaningful way.

Many US states have higher minimum-wage requirements than the government, with Washington State leading the pack at $9.19 an hour. That's a start, but many large, international companies will only pay the minimum the federal government requires. As a result, the federal minimum wage keeps an entire class of people trapped in economic servitude, focusing their attention on survival rather than growth, barring their ability to save enough or pay for education that would allow them to rise to the middle class.

Income inequality is as bad as it has ever been—and the reason is simple.

Low-wage workers can't even care for their own health without giving up some other necessity. According to the Center for Economic and Policy Research, it took a minimum-wage worker 130 hours to earn a year's worth of health benefits in 1979. That is only three-and-a-half weeks of full-time, minimum-wage work. By 2011, the same health coverage cost 749 hours, or 19 weeks of full-time, minimum-wage work. Working nearly half the year to afford only healthcare, and nothing else, is a ridiculous demand to make of low-wage workers.

The low minimum wage is also as costly for the government as it is cheap for companies. While McDonald's or other fast food companies save pennies and boost their profitability by paying a low wage, their workers cannot survive on that amount and often end up taking welfare benefits. In 2012, 4.3 million people received welfare benefits and 47 million received food stamps. The number of Americans getting food stamps—a national hunger crisis—has risen in tandem with the number of people unemployed or out of the workforce.

The minimum-wage salary is eaten up fast by necessities like food and healthcare: US minimum-wage workers don't just lack cash; they lack benefits, and this ends up costing the government. Each of the 23 million households on food stamps is getting an average benefit of about $274 a month from the government to pay for meals. About 40% of food stamp recipients live in a household where at least one person is earning money, according to the US Department of Agriculture.

That means that the money being spent on food stamps is money that the government is paying to subsidize company profits: as businesses pay a minimum or near-minimum wage, their workers are forced to turn to government programs to make ends meet. There is, as they say, no such thing as a free lunch.

Analyst Sarah Millar, of ConvergEx, points out that the US is among the worst nations in providing benefits for low-paid workers:

> What the minimum wage debate seems to be missing … is the dialogue that focuses on benefits as the missing element of compensation rather than higher pay. The minimum wage debate is misdirected—among both the workers demanding higher wages and the politicians struggling to determine the minimum wage. Simply put, the problem is not wages: it's total compensation—that is, wages and benefits.
>
> Where we deviate from the norm is on directly-paid benefits: only 9% of US wages are paid out in the form of benefits, compared to a 16.2% average for the 30 countries surveyed by the BLS. We're 29th out of 30. That puts us below developing countries like Brazil and Estonia, and far behind developed

nations like Japan—which has very similar minimum and manufacturing wages.

The latest Bureau of Labor Statistics employee benefit survey illuminates how minimum-wage workers make just enough money to survive, but nothing more. Just over a tenth of low-paid workers participated in any kind of healthcare benefits, for instance, and roughly the same amount had life insurance or participated in any kind of retirement plan. One-fifth took sick leave, and only 39% took any kind of vacation.

It's also more expensive to be poor than it is to be middle-class or rich. If low-wage workers do want to have healthcare, they pay more, relative to their salaries, for medical care premiums. Obamacare is supposed to reverse this, but implementation has been held up.

A pathologically useless Congress won't pass any minimum-wage legislation, no matter how the president asks for it. But as dysfunctional as the budget conversation is, this is the right time for a discussion of the premises of our society. Do we want to be a society that ignores the unemployment crisis and looks away from the fact that the majority of "job growth" right now is in low-wage jobs? Do we want to be a country that expects to let millions of people fail economically in the mistaken belief that there will be no wider consequences to the rest of us?

It's time to get real. Allowing the federal minimum wage to be so low means knowing that it will cost us all in Medicare, food stamp and social security payments later. While some in Congress—particularly on the conservative side—have mistakenly insisted on austerity and complained about the rising cost of federal benefits, they also seem not to have done the math to figure out why those costs are going up.

The solution is simple: raise the minimum wage, add benefits, and so reduce government benefit spending. If the minimum wage remains low, and benefits sparse, government spending on benefits will continue to rise.

These questions are ever more relevant—in the economic recovery "that isn't." Low-wage jobs are becoming the new normal, and they're creeping up the generational spectrum: about 43% of minimum-wage jobs are in the food industry, which used to employ mostly teenagers, but now employs adults. Maybe these employers should start paying people like adults, too.

Raising the minimum wage will boost the economy. But just as importantly, so would adding benefits. If America wants to reclaim the mantle of economic leadership, this is how to do it.

Periodical and Internet Sources Bibliography

The following articles have been selected to supplement the diverse views presented in this chapter.

Ben Casselman and Kathryn Casteel, "Seattle's Minimum Wage Hike May Have Gone Too Far," FiveThirtyEight, June 26, 2017. https://fivethirtyeight.com/features/seattles-minimum-wage-hike-may-have-gone-too-far.

Pascal-Emmanuel Gobry, "An Alternative to Increasing the Minimum Wage," *National Review*, February 16, 2017. https://www.nationalreview.com/2017/02/minimum-wage-increase-conservatives.

Steven Greenhouse, "Fight for $15 Movement Plans Fast Food Workers' Strike Across South," *Guardian*, February 1, 2018. https://www.theguardian.com/us-news/2018/feb/01/fight-for-15-movement-plans-fast-food-workers-strike-across-south.

Isobel Asher Hamilton and Jake Kanter, "Amazon's Minimum-Wage Hike Barely Made a Dent in Its Operating Costs, and It May Explain Why Some Workers Say They're Actually Earning Less," *Business Insider*, February 1, 2019. https://www.businessinsider.com/amazon-minimum-wage-hike-barely-made-a-dent-in-its-operating-costs-2019-2.

Sheela Kolhatkar, "Walmart and the Push to Put Workers on Company Boards," *New Yorker*, March 26, 2019. https://www.newyorker.com/business/currency/walmart-and-the-push-to-put-workers-on-company-boards.

Juleyka Lantigua-Williams, "Raise the Minimum Wage, Reduce Crime? A New White House Report Links Higher Hourly Incomes to Lower Rates of Law-Breaking," *Atlantic*, May 3, 2016. https://www.theatlantic.com/politics/archive/2016/05/raise-the-minimum-wage-reduce-crime/480912.

Jacob Pramuk, "Democrats Introduce Bill to Hike Federal Minimum Wage to $15 per Hour," CNBC, January 16, 2019. https://www.cnbc.com/2019/01/16/house-democrats-introduce-bill-to-hike-minimum-wage-to-15-per-hour.html.

Hamza Shaban, "McDonald's Says It's Done Lobbying Against Raising the Minimum Wage," *Washington Post*, March 27, 2019. https://www.washingtonpost.com/business/2019/03/27/mcdonalds-says-its-done-lobbying-against-raising-minimum-wage/?utm_term=.8b9120badf8f.

Katrina Vanden Heuvel, "The 'Best Economy' Ever Isn't Working for Working People," *Nation*, April 2, 2019. https://www.thenation.com/article/the-best-economy-ever-isnt-working-for-working-people.

For Further Discussion

Chapter 1

1. This chapter describes several ways unions have benefitted workers, even when those workers were not in unions. Why do you think these benefits to the larger working community haven't created more widespread support for unions?
2. One author argues that declining support for unions is in fact due to the remarkable successes of unions in years past. Does this suggest that unions have become obsolete? Why or why not?

Chapter 2

1. This chapter contains an argument that increased unionization would help end the recession that was underway at the time the article was written. What effect do you think increased unionization would have now?
2. One viewpoint in this chapter quotes a scholar as saying, "American business was at its most productive and powerful at the time when there was a high percentage of unionized workers." If this is true, why do you think businesses go to such pains to prevent their workers from forming unions?

Chapter 3

1. One of this chapter's authors refers to something called "works councils," a system common in some European countries in which workers have a say in the decision making of the businesses they work for. Is this a good idea? Why or why not?
2. The term right-to-work legislation seems misleading—since it neither gives nor denies anyone the right to work. Why do you think it has been called that?

Chapter 4

1. Why do workers need the right to bargain collectively with employers? Why does that right need to be protected and what is it being protected from?
2. Do you think that Libertarians and Republicans have different reasons for being anti-union and pro-right-to-work legislation? If so, what are these reasons?

Chapter 5

1. One author in this chapter points out that many companies cut hours and increase automation when faced with mandated minimum wage increases. He cites studies showing an increase in automation in the workplace. How strong do you think this connection is? Do you think companies would not automate if they could pay humans lower wages?
2. Several of the viewpoints in this chapter refer to the moral arguments for increasing the minimum wage—basically that it is wrong to pay people less than a living wage while the companies they work for make large profits. Do you think this is a valid argument? Why or why not?

Organizations to Contact

The editors have compiled the following list of organizations concerned with the issues debated in this book. The descriptions are derived from materials provided by the organizations. All have publications or information available for interested readers. The list was compiled on the date of publication of the present volume; the information provided here may change. Be aware that many organizations take several weeks or longer to respond to inquiries, so allow as much time as possible.

AFL-CIO (The American Federation of Labor and Congress of Industrial Organizations)

815 16th St NW
Washington, DC 20006
(202) 637-5018
email: contact via website form
website: www.aflcio.org

The AFL-CIO is a democratic, voluntary federation of 55 national and international labor unions representing 12.5 million working men and women. Their goal is to ensure all working people are treated fairly, with decent paychecks and benefits, safe jobs, dignity, and equal opportunities.

Center for American Progress

1333 H Street NW, 10th Floor
Washington, DC 20005
(202) 682-1611
email: contact via website form
website: www.americanprogress.org

The Center for American Progress is a nonpartisan policy institute dedicated to improving the lives of Americans through bold ideas, leadership, and action.

Change to Win: Strategic Organizing Center

1900 L Street NW
Suite 900
Washington, DC 20036
(202) 721-0660
email: info@changetowin.org
website: www.changetowin.org

Change to Win is a federation of labor organizations representing over five million working men and women.

Coalition of Black Trade Unionists

1155 Connecticut Avenue, Suite 500
Washington, DC 20036
(202) 778-3318
email: cbtu@cbtu.org
website: www.cbtu.org

The CBTU is an affiliate member of the AFL-CIO representing black workers in the trade union movement.

Coalition of Labor Union Women

815 16th Street NW
Washington, DC 20006
email: contact via website form
website: www.cluw.org

CLUW, a non-partisan labor organization, is America's only national organization for union women.

Fight for $15

email: info@fightfor15.org
website: www.fightfor15.org

Fight for $15 is a grass-roots organization of underpaid workers working to increase the minimum wage.

Interfaith Worker Justice

1020 W. Bryn Mawr Avenue
Chicago, IL 60660
(773) 728-8400
email: contact via web form
website: www.iwj.org

This network of workers is dedicated to addressing the root causes of widespread economic disparity and indignity in the workplace.

National Right to Work Legal Defense and Education Foundation

8001 Braddock Road
Springfield, VA 22160
(703) 321-8510
email: pts@nrtw.org
website: www.nrtw.org

This nonprofit organization strives to eliminate compulsory unionism through litigation, information, and education.

United Association for Labor Education

PO Box 14655
Portland, OR 97293-0655
(503) 704-3845
email: contact via web form
website: www.uale.org

The UALE is an organization that supports labor educators in attempts to develop new leadership and strengthen the field of labor education.

William Brennan Institute for Labor Studies (WBILS)

6001 Dodge Street, 115E CEC
Omaha, NE 68182
(402) 554-5902
email unowbils@unomaha.edu
website: www.unomaha.edu/college-of-public-affairs-and
-community-service/william-brennan-institute-for-labor
-studies/

A project of the College of Public Affairs and Community Service at the University of Nebraska, Omaha, WBILS aims to foster creative and critical thinking among labor leaders, future labor leaders, and union members.

Bibliography of Books

William M. Adler. *The Man Who Never Died: The Life, Times, and Legacy of Joe Hill, American Labor Icon*. New York, NY: Bloomsbury, 2012.

Paul Buhle and Steve Max (authors), and Noah Van Sciver (illustrator). *Eugene V. Debs: A Graphic Biography*. New York, NY: Verso, 2019.

Jefferson Cowie. *Stayin' Alive: The 1970s and the Last Days of the Working Class*. New York, NY: The New Press, 2010.

Philip Dray. *There Is Power in a Union: The Epic Story of Labor in America*. New York, NY: Anchor, 2011.

Melvyn Dubofsky and Joseph A. McCartin. *Labor in America: A History* (Ninth edition). Malden, MA: John Wiley & Sons, 2017.

Rosemary Feurer and Chad Pearson, eds. *Against Labor: How US Employers Organized to Defeat Union Activism*. Urbana, IL: University of Illinois Press, 2017.

Thomas Geoghegan. *Only One Thing Can Save Us: Why America Needs a New Kind of Labor Movement*. New York, NY: New Press, 2016.

Elliott J. Gorn. *Mother Jones: The Most Dangerous Woman in America*. New York, NY: Hill and Wang, 2015.

Steven Greenhouse. *Beaten Down, Worked Up: The Past, Present, and Future of American Labor*. New York, NY: Knopf, 2019.

Raymond L. Hogler. *The End of American Labor Unions: The Right to Work Movement and the Erosion of Collective Bargaining*. Santa Barbara, CA: Praeger, 2015.

Jill Lepore. *These Truths: A History of the United States*. New York, NY: W. W. Norton, 2018.

Erik Loomis. *A History of America in Ten Strikes*. New York, NY: The New Press, 2018.

Priscilla Murolo and A. B. Chitty. *From the Folks Who Brought You the Weekend: A Short Illustrated History of Labor in the United States*. New York, NY: The New Press, 2018.

AnneLise Orleck. *We Are All Fast-Food Workers Now: The Global Uprising Against Poverty Wages*. Boston, MA: Beacon Press, 2018.

Lane Windham. *Knocking on Labor's Door: Union Organizing in the 1970s and the Roots of a New Economic Divide*. Chapel Hill, NC: University of North Carolina Press, 2017.

Index

OPPOSING VIEWPOINTS® SERIES

Labor Unions and Workers' Rights

Other Books of Related Interest

Opposing Viewpoints Series

Automation of Labor
Identity Politics
Uber, Lyft, Airbnb, and the Sharing Economy
The Wealth Gap

At Issue Series

Civil Disobedience
Political Corruption
Public Outrage and Protest
The Right to a Living Wage

Current Controversies Series

Fair Trade
Globalization
Tariffs and the Future of Trade
Whistleblowers